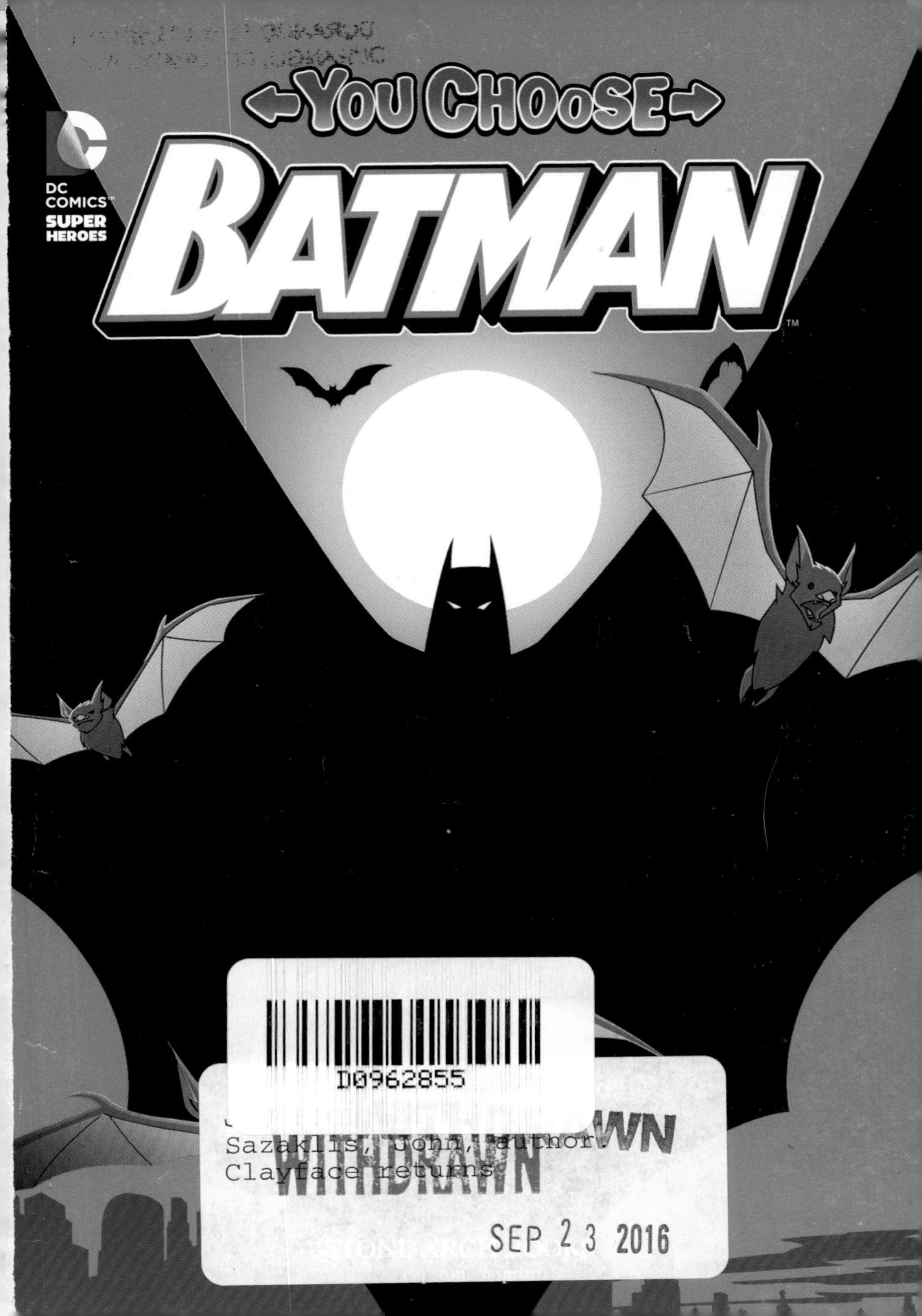
YOU CHOOSE
BATMAN
DC COMICS SUPER HEROES

You Choose Stories: Batman
is published by Stone Arch Books,
A Capstone Imprint
1710 Roe Crest Drive
North Mankato, Minnesota 56003
www.mycapstone.com

STAR35566

Cataloging-in-Publication Data is available
on the Library of Congress website.
ISBN: 978-1-4965-3089-9 (library binding)
ISBN: 978-1-4965-3091-2 (paperback)
ISBN: 978-1-4965-3093-6 (eBook pdf)

Summary: Years ago actor Matt Hagen's career was ruined
when he became the monstrous Clayface. Now he's back
for revenge! Only you can help Batman track down and
stop the dangerous shape-shifter in Clayface Returns!

Printed and bound in Canada.
009631F16

←YOU CHOOSE→

BATMAN ™

CLAYFACE RETURNS

Batman created by Bob Kane with Bill Finger

written by
John Sazaklis

illustrated by
Ethen Beavers

←YOU CHOOSE→
BATMAN™

The menacing mudman is back!
Clayface is seeking his revenge on crooked
businessman Roland Daggett, and only YOU
can help stop him. With your help, the Dark
Knight can track down and put a stop to the
shape-shifter's plans in *Clayface Returns*!

Follow the directions at the bottom
of each page. The choices YOU make will
change the outcome of the story. After you
finish one path, go back and read the others
for more Batman adventures!

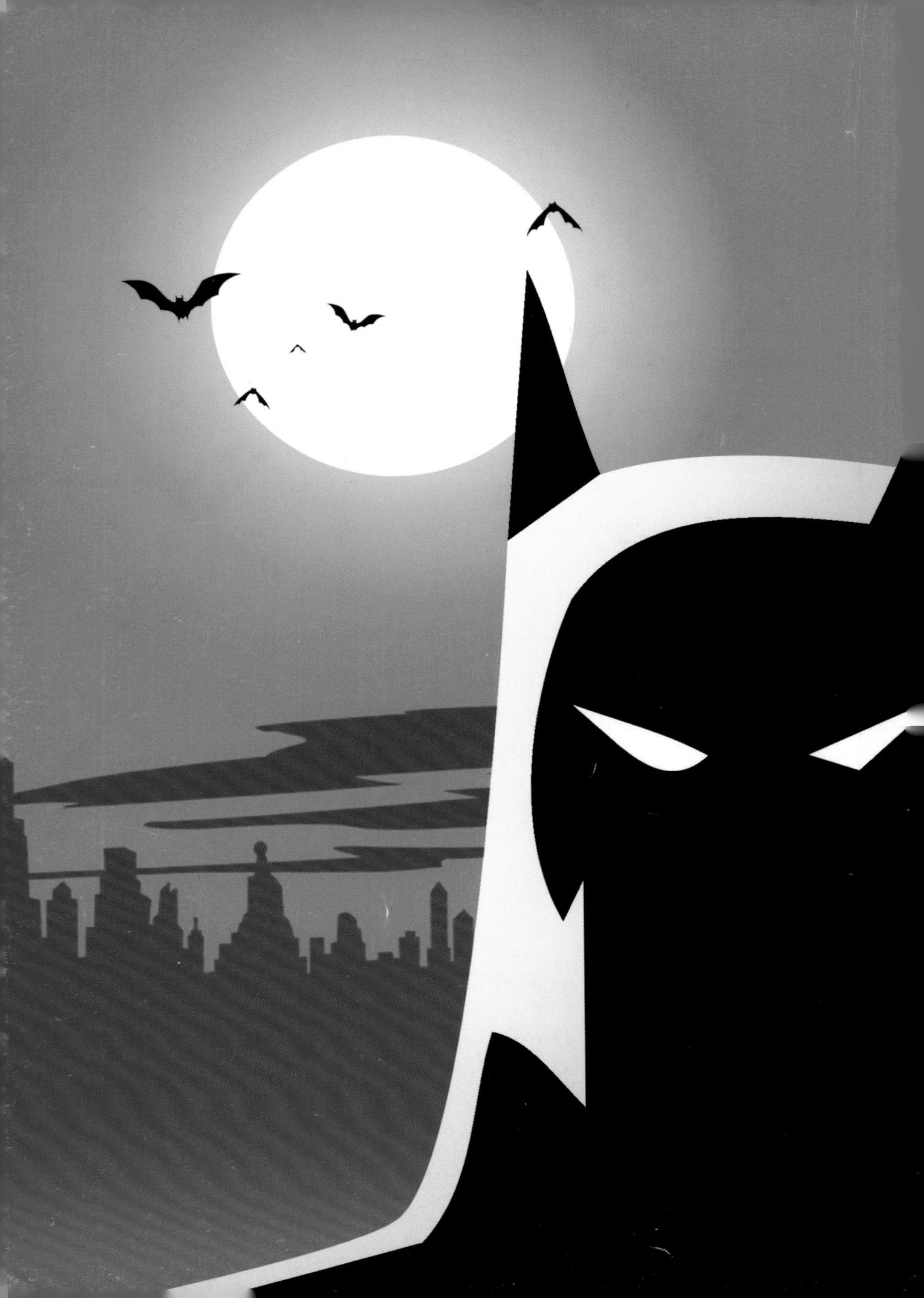

KRA-KOOM!

It is a dark and stormy night in Gotham City. Heavy rain falls down in sheets as bolts of lightning slice through the darkness. A sleek black vehicle streaks through the puddled streets. Bystanders stop in awe at the sight of the armored car.

"The Batmobile!" someone gasps.

The Batmobile belongs to Batman, the Dark Knight of Gotham City and the World's Greatest Detective. He's investigating the recent kidnapping of Mayor Hamilton Hill.

Batman speaks into a monitor on the Batmobile's dash. "All the clues lead to the old clock tower on the roof of the Town Hall building, Alfred," he says.

Alfred Pennyworth is a gray-haired gentleman with a black mustache, and Batman's loyal butler. "Yes, I did read the article about the Mayor calling for the demolition of the clock tower, sir," Alfred recalls. "It was the day before his disappearance."

Turn the page.

"We know of one criminal with a clock obsession, as well as a huge grudge against Mayor Hill," Batman states.

"The Clock King!" exclaims Alfred.

"Precisely, old friend," says Batman. "And time is of the essence. Let's hope I'm not too late!"

Batman pulls up in front of Town Hall. The building's main feature is the huge clock at the top.

A flash of lightning outlines the silhouette of a man standing near the clock. "SAVE THE CLOCK TOWER!" shouts the man from above.

"I've got the Clock King in my sights, Alfred," Batman says. "Over and out."

"Good luck, sir," Alfred replies.

The Dark Knight exits the Batmobile. He aims his grapnel gun at one of the clock's hands and fires. *PAF!*

A steel cable shoots into the air. The hook at the end grips the large metal minute hand. The cable retracts, hoisting Batman into the air.

WHOOSH!

The Caped Crusader lands on a ledge next to the clock tower.

"Good evening, Batman," crows the Clock King. He takes a bow and tips his bowler hat at Batman. "You're just in time for your doom!"

"Where is Mayor Hill?" Batman growls.

"Oh, he's a little tied up at the moment!" laughs the villain.

Inside the tower, large metal gears grind and squeal. **CREEEAAK!** The mayor is gagged and tied to the large moving part—it's about to roll into another huge gear!

"Looks like Mayor Hill's term will expire sooner than expected!" the Clock King sneers.

Batman leaps into the tower and rushes toward the mayor.

"First things first, Batman," the villain says, thrusting a sword at the hero. "Back to your regularly scheduled death, already in progress!"

The Caped Crusader backflips out of harm's way.

Turn the page.

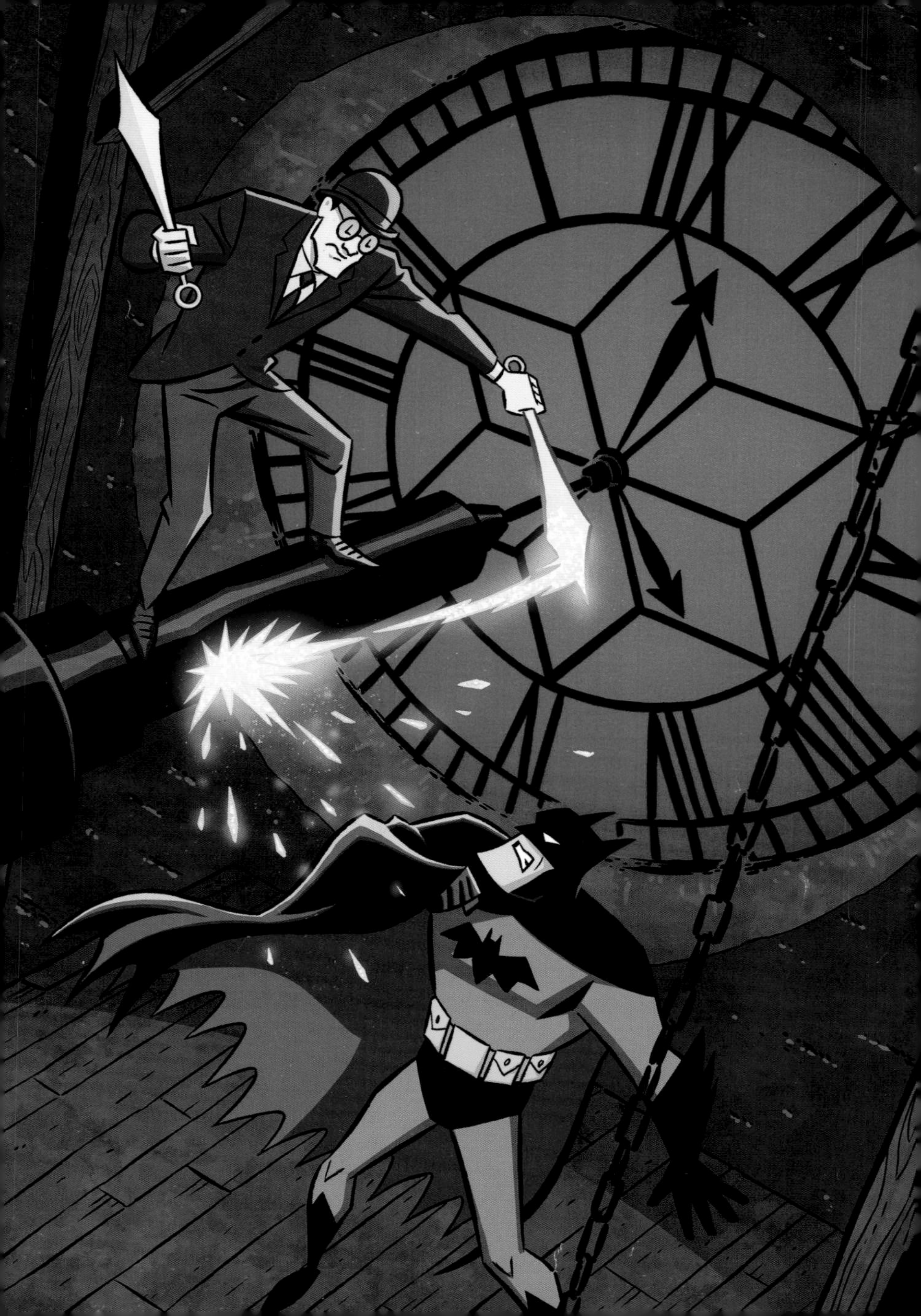

The Clock King presses forward, scraping his weapons along the huge gears inside the giant clock. **SKREEEUNCH!!** Batman uses his cape to shield himself from the shower of sparks.

"Why are you doing this?" Batman growls.

"It's all quite simple, really!" shouts the Clock King. "The clock tower is a historical landmark. The mayor plans to tear it down, and I plan to stop him by any means necessary."

The villain cackles with glee as he swipes his blades at the Dark Knight. Batman produces two Batarangs from his Utility Belt. He hurls them at the Clock King, knocking the swords from his hands. **CLANK! CLANK!**

"OUCH!" the Clock King yelps.

Batman kicks the Clock King to the ground, then aims and shoots his grapnel gun toward the rafters. **PFFT-THUNK!**

The hook grabs onto a wooden rafter and Batman hoists himself up. He grips the nearest gear tightly and crawls over it to reach Mayor Hill.

Turn the page.

"Time waits for no man, Caped Crusader," the Clock King says, getting back on his feet. "You're in quite the literal time crunch, aren't you?"

The heavy prongs of the gear inch closer, bringing with them certain doom!

Batman pulls out a sharpened Batarang and slices through the thick ropes holding the mayor. With seconds to spare, the Caped Crusader grabs the mayor and carries him to safety.

"Curses! You foiled my perfect plot!" shouts the Clock King. "It's time for my exit!" The villain then rushes to escape.

"Not so fast," growls Batman. In a flash, he snares the Clock King with his Batrope.

"Your time is up," the hero states. "You'll be spending the foreseeable future in Arkham Asylum."

Batman contacts the police with the communicator in his cowl. Within minutes, the dawn sky is pulsing with red and blue police lights. Commissioner Gordon and his team soon surround the Town Hall building.

"Well, at least they're prompt," Clock King grumbles.

"We got your message, Batman," the commissioner says. "Thank you for your help."

"And thank you for saving my life," Mayor Hill adds.

"You're welcome," Batman replies. "Now you must do your part to save the clock tower. I believe that billionaire Bruce Wayne will be making a large donation to fund its repair. It's up to you to make sure it's preserved as a historical landmark."

The Clock King is surprised, but satisfied. He cooperates with the officers as they take him to a nearby squad car.

"Well, that was a little nerve-wracking," the mayor says to Commissioner Gordon. "It feels like an election year! Batman, will I be getting your vote?"

When the men turn around for an answer, the Caped Crusader is already gone.

Turn the page.

Batman drives the Batmobile to the outskirts of Gotham City. He enters his secret hideout known as the Batcave. It is filled with advanced, state-of-the-art crime-fighting equipment.

The Batcave also includes a trophy room where Batman keeps souvenirs from his cases. After this mission, the Clock King's hour hand sword is going on display. Batman places it between Mr. Freeze's freeze gun and the Riddler's question mark cane.

Batman pulls off his mask to reveal his secret identity, that of billionaire Bruce Wayne. He makes his way upstairs into the study of Wayne Manor. Alfred has prepared a wonderful breakfast.

"Good morning, sir," Alfred says. "Time to recharge your batteries."

"Ha! You sound just like the Clock King," Bruce says, clapping the butler on the back.

Alfred smiles and pours Bruce a glass of orange juice. Just then, young Tim Drake comes bounding into the room. Tim is Bruce's current ward, as well as Batman's sidekick—Robin, the Boy Wonder!

"Today's the day!" Tim cheers. "The first day of the Gotham City World's Fair!"

"How could I forget, Tim?" Bruce replies. "I've been waiting for it all year. I'm actually thrilled to see Simon Trent. He played the Gray Ghost!"

"Who?" Tim asks.

"The Gray Ghost was my favorite show when I was a kid. It's partly why I became a crime fighter."

Bruce grins from ear to ear. "Mr. Trent is making an appearance at the Auto Pavilion, alongside his high-tech car from the TV show!"

"Then what are we waiting for?" Tim says. "Let's go!"

After breakfast, Alfred drives Bruce and Tim to the fair near the Gotham City Harbor. Outside the futuristic event center, Tim picks up a program and flips through it.

"Hey, Bruce," Tim says, "it looks like the Gray Ghost isn't making his appearance until this afternoon. There's plenty of time to check out some other cool stuff."

Turn the page.

When the duo enter the building, they see a gleaming booth in the center. The words *ReNuYu Too* are on a big banner overhead.

"*ReNuYu* was a poisonous product created by Roland Daggett," Bruce says. "He was jailed years ago for his corrupt schemes. But now he's out on parole."

"Looks like he's selling a new version. The sign claims it's the '*Face of the Future!*'" Tim replies.

"'*Face of the Future*'?" Bruce asks. "Let me tell you about a face from the past ..."

Just then Bruce sees a large banner for *ZATANNA: MISTRESS OF MAGIC!*

"Zatanna!" exclaims Bruce.

"Who's that?" Tim asks.

"A marvelously talented magician, and one of my oldest friends," says Bruce. "It would be great to see her again!"

If the duo investigates Daggett's new product, turn to page 18.

If Bruce and Tim wait for the Gray Ghost at the Auto Pavilion, turn to page 23.

If they watch Zatanna's magic show, turn to page 35.

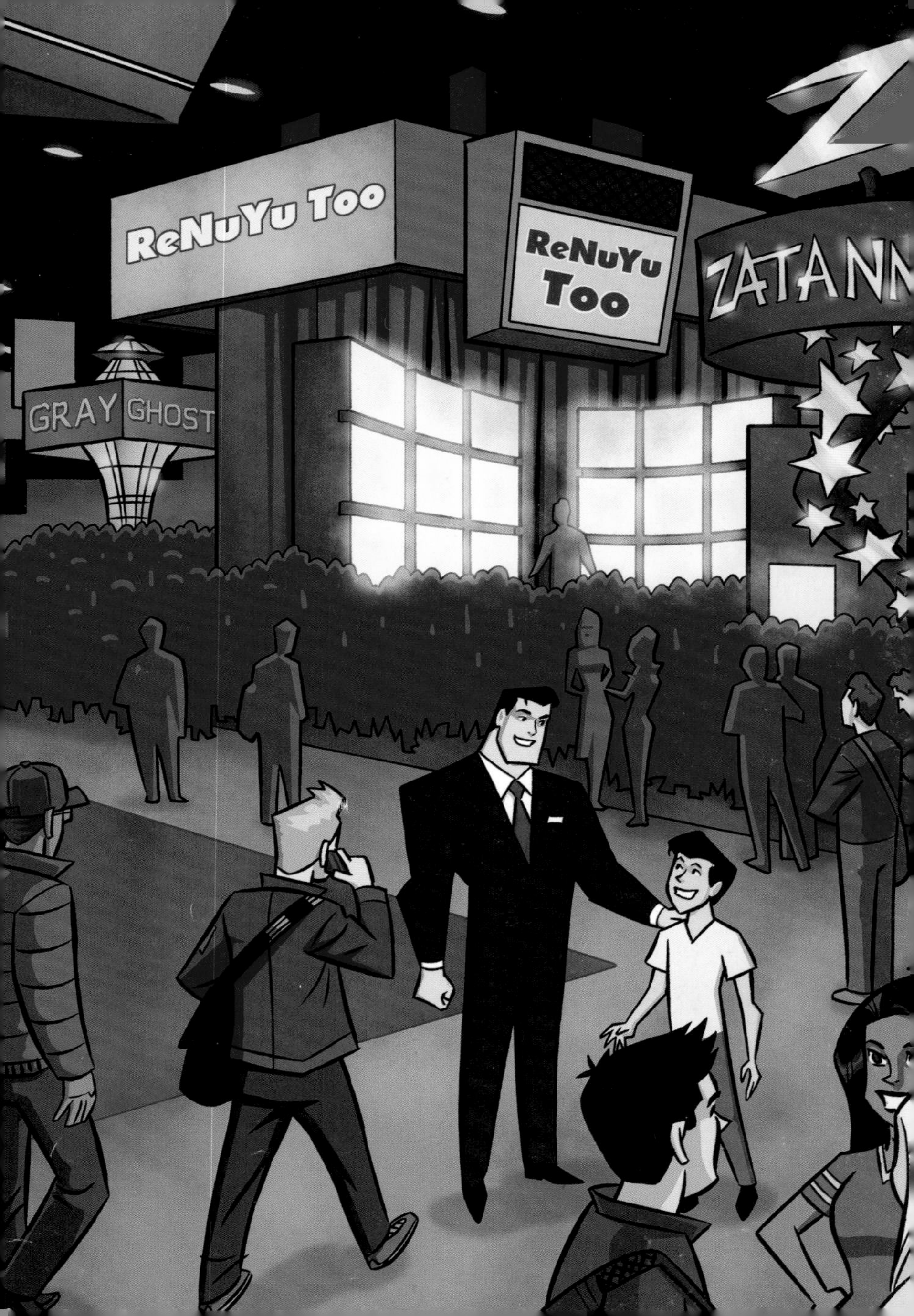
ReNuYu Too
ReNuYu Too
ZATANN
GRAY GHOST

With a determined stride, Bruce heads toward the *ReNuYu Too* booth.

"So, what's the story with Daggett?" Tim asks.

"Years ago, Daggett developed his product, pronounced '*Renew You.*' He claimed it could instantly restore youthful good looks," Bruce says.

"Around the same time, successful movie star Matt Hagen was in a terrible car accident. It ruined his handsome features. Hagen's hospital bills ate away at his fortune and the actor turned to Daggett for help," Bruce continues.

"Do you think Daggett is up to his old schemes?" Tim asks.

"Wherever Daggett is, trouble is sure to follow," Bruce replies. "You see, the *ReNuYu* cream allowed Hagen to change his face into anything he wanted. But he became addicted to it. When he couldn't pay for more, Daggett bribed him to commit crimes in exchange for the product. Ultimately, Hagen fell victim to an overdose of the chemical—and was transformed into the shape-changing villain known as Clayface!"

"Clayface!" Tim gasps. "We haven't seen him or any of his shape-shifting shenanigans in a long time."

"Too long," Bruce says.

When Bruce and Tim reach the booth, several people surround it. In the middle of the crowd stands shady businessman Roland Daggett.

"Step right up, folks! Step right up!" he announces. "*ReNuYu* Too will make you feel like a billion bucks! Don't believe me? Just listen to our new spokesmodel!"

Daggett steps aside and makes a grand gesture to the enormous screen behind him. The screen flickers to life and a picture comes into focus. It is the smiling face of a very handsome man—Bruce Wayne!

"What's going on here, Bruce?" Tim asks, stunned.

"I don't know," Bruce replies. "But I do know that things are not what they seem."

If Bruce confronts Daggett, turn to page 20.
If Bruce and Tim watch the presentation, turn to page 29.

The lights dim as the presentation starts. Loud music blares through the speakers as Bruce and Tim push through the crowd. Finally, the billionaire is face to face with the slimy businessman.

"What's your game, Daggett?" Bruce asks sternly. "I did not agree to have my likeness used for your profit."

"HA!" Daggett laughs. "It was YOUR idea. You came to me and begged to do it because you needed the money."

Bruce takes a step back, stunned from the accusation.

Daggett straightens his tie, brushes past Bruce, and walks onto the stage. "Don't worry, pretty boy," Daggett calls over his shoulder. "Your check's in the mail."

Suddenly, a woman in the crowd shrieks. "Oh, my gosh, it's BRUCE WAYNE!"

The crowd focuses its attention on Bruce and clamors around him. People take out their phones and start snapping pictures. Annoyed, the billionaire quickly walks away from the booth.

"I hate when that happens," Bruce says.

"Yeah, too bad," Tim replies. "If only you had some sort of mask to cover your face so people wouldn't recognize you ..."

The crowd from the booth catches up to the duo. "Mr. Wayne!" one man cries out. "I'm a big fan!"

"Mr. Wayne!" another one shouts. "Can I get an autograph?"

"Oh, Brucie!" a woman calls. "How about a kiss!?"

"Let's get out of here fast!" Bruce says.

Bruce and Tim sprint out of the show floor and bolt to the nearest exit. The screaming fans give chase. But thanks to their peak physical condition, they easily outrun the eager admirers.

Turn the page.

Bruce pushes the emergency door open and the two friends find themselves in a narrow hallway. The door slams shut behind them, locking them out of the pavilion. *BAM!*

"We must solve this mystery of mistaken identity ... but as Batman and Robin," Bruce says.

Bruce and Tim move to another door at the end of the hall. They try it but it won't budge. "This one is locked too," Bruce says.

"We're trapped in a dead end," Tim replies. "Think you can pick the lock?"

"Sorry, I left those tools in my other belt," quips Bruce.

"What are we going to do?"

"I'm going to call Alfred. He'll find a staff member and have them get us out," Bruce sighs. "I can't believe we're stuck here. Daggett's going to get away with whatever corrupt scheme he's planning!"

THE END

To follow another path, turn to page 16.

Excited, Bruce and Tim go to the Auto Pavilion. "I can't wait to see Simon Trent," Bruce says. "I had all the Gray Ghost toys as a kid. I hope I can get his autograph."

All around the show floor are vehicles from the past and present, as well as models of future vehicles.

"These rides are sweet!" Tim cries. "Maybe not as sweet as the one we have …" Bruce smiles at the thought of the Batmobile.

Through the crowd, the duo sees a familiar face. It's Police Commissioner Gordon. "Hello, Commissioner," Bruce says, shaking the man's hand. "Is everything all right?"

"Everything is fine," the Commissioner replies. "I'm enjoying my day off with my daughter Barbara." A young, red-haired woman walks over holding two buckets of popcorn.

"Hi, everybody!" she says cheerfully. "Are you here to see the Gray Ghost too? Daddy's been talking about it for weeks!" Commissioner Gordon blushes.

Turn the page.

The four friends walk toward a large stage with a red velvet curtain. Just then, an announcer's voice booms over the loudspeakers. "Ladies and gentleman," it says. "We are happy to present the Auto Pavilion's main attraction!"

The lights dim and the curtain rises. There is a round of applause as the spotlight lands on the Gray Ghost's sleek silver car. Its polished chrome glints under the lights.

Bruce lets out a low whistle. "Impressive," he says.

"Most of you know it as the famous vehicle driven by legendary TV hero, the Gray Ghost!" the voice continues. "Please welcome the Gray Ghost himself—Mr. Simon Trent!"

Simon Trent walks onto the stage in his full Gray Ghost costume—a tailored suit, long flowing cape, fedora hat, and goggles. All the items are different shades of gray.

"Greetings, citizens!" the Gray Ghost says. He waves and the crowd goes wild. "It's a pleasure to be here in Gotham City!"

Tim and Barbara whip out their phones and start snapping pictures.

"I'm a bit embarrassed to admit this, Mr. Wayne, but I'm a huge fan of his," Commissioner Gordon says to Bruce.

"Don't worry, Commissioner, you're not the only one," Bruce replies. "How about we get a better look?"

As the two men walk closer to the stage, the Gray Ghost pats the hood of his car.

"Isn't she a beauty?" he asks. "We've had a lot of adventures together!" The actor receives another round of applause from the fans.

But suddenly, a dark shadow falls across the stage, blocking the Gray Ghost's spotlight!

Turn the page.

Everyone in the room looks up. Some people gasp. One person screams.

A dark, pointy-eared figure swoops by overhead and lands on the stage next to the startled Gray Ghost. A black cape billows around him.

WHOOSH!

"It's Batman!" somebody shouts. The crowd cheers even more.

"Batman?!" Tim and Bruce both exclaim. They exchange nervous looks.

"I didn't know the Caped Crusader took part in publicity stunts," Commissioner Gordon says.

"He doesn't," Bruce says, visibly annoyed.

"Hey there, Batman!" the Gray Ghost says with a nervous chuckle. "I wasn't expecting you to make an appearance. Glad you could join us!"

The Caped Crusader narrows his eyes. "This show's over!" he sneers.

If Bruce and Tim watch what happens next, go to page 27.

If Bruce and Tim change into Batman and Robin, turn to page 40.

Bruce and Tim watch the mysterious Batman advance menacingly toward the Gray Ghost. He leaves a trail of muddy footprints across the stage.

"Gray Ghost, you're coming with me," Batman says.

The Caped Crusader grabs the actor roughly by his shirt. Then he takes out his grapnel gun and fires it into the rafters above.

SHOOM!

In a flash, the two men are propelled through the air. They land on a catwalk overlooking the show floor.

"The Gray Ghost is now my prisoner!" Batman shouts. "If you want to see him alive, stay tuned for my ransom instructions!"

Then he picks up the actor and disappears from sight.

Turn the page.

The onlookers are stunned. "Did you see what Batman just did?" one of them asks.

Commissioner Gordon speaks into his police radio. "Calling all available units," he barks. "Be on the lookout for Batman. I can't believe I'm saying this, but he just kidnapped the Gray Ghost!"

Bruce and Tim look at each other. "Clearly that man was an impostor," Bruce says.

"Who could it be?" the teen asks.

Bruce and Tim climb onto the stage. They kneel down to examine some muddy footprints.

"This compound is a mixture of dirt and clay," Bruce says grimly.

"Clay!" Tim exclaims. "There's only one villain we know of with those shape-changing abilities."

"Precisely," Bruce replies. "I'm afraid the Gray Ghost is in grave danger."

"Oh, no!" cries Tim. "He's in the clutches of Clayface … and we let him get away!"

THE END

To follow another path, turn to page 16.

Classical music pumps in from the speakers. A video starts to play on the digital display. The viewers watch as Bruce Wayne addresses the audience.

"It's no secret that I'm a handsome billionaire and philanthropist," the man on screen says with a charming smile. "But there is a secret to my dashing good looks ... and I'm going to share it with you!"

Holding up a fancy bottle, he says, "It's *ReNuYu Too*, the new and improved face cream from Daggett Industries. It will make you look and feel like a billion bucks!"

As the video ends, the picture freezes on Bruce Wayne's smiling face. The crowd cheers and claps. But the real Bruce Wayne is steamed. "I never filmed that commercial," he says to Tim. "Nor did I give them permission to use my likeness."

Turn the page.

"What are you going to do?" Tim asks.

"Confront Daggett and get to the bottom of this sham!" Bruce states.

Bruce marches toward the stage. But before he can get to Daggett, the bold businessman picks up a microphone.

"Ladies and gentlemen, Daggett Industries has a very special announcement! Our special spokesman is here in person to meet and greet every one of you," he announces. "Let's give a round of applause to the one and only Golden Boy of Gotham City, Mr. Bruce Wayne!"

Just then, a man that looks exactly like Bruce Wayne walks onto the stage and waves at the crowd. Behind him is a trail of muddy footprints.

"Whoa!" Tim says with a whistle. "I must be seeing double."

If Bruce confronts the impostor, go to page 31.
If Bruce and Tim leave to become Batman and Robin, turn to page 55.

"We need to put an end to this double trouble," Bruce replies through clenched teeth.

Bruce weaves his way through the crowd and nimbly jumps onto the stage. Daggett is startled by his presence and does a double take. He is standing between two identical Bruce Waynes!

The crowd gasps, and the businessman chuckles nervously. Sweat pours from his brow.

"Ladies and gentlemen," he says. "Looks like you get two for the price of one today!"

The real Bruce pushes past Daggett and confronts his double.

"Who are you and what do you want?" he demands.

Turn the page.

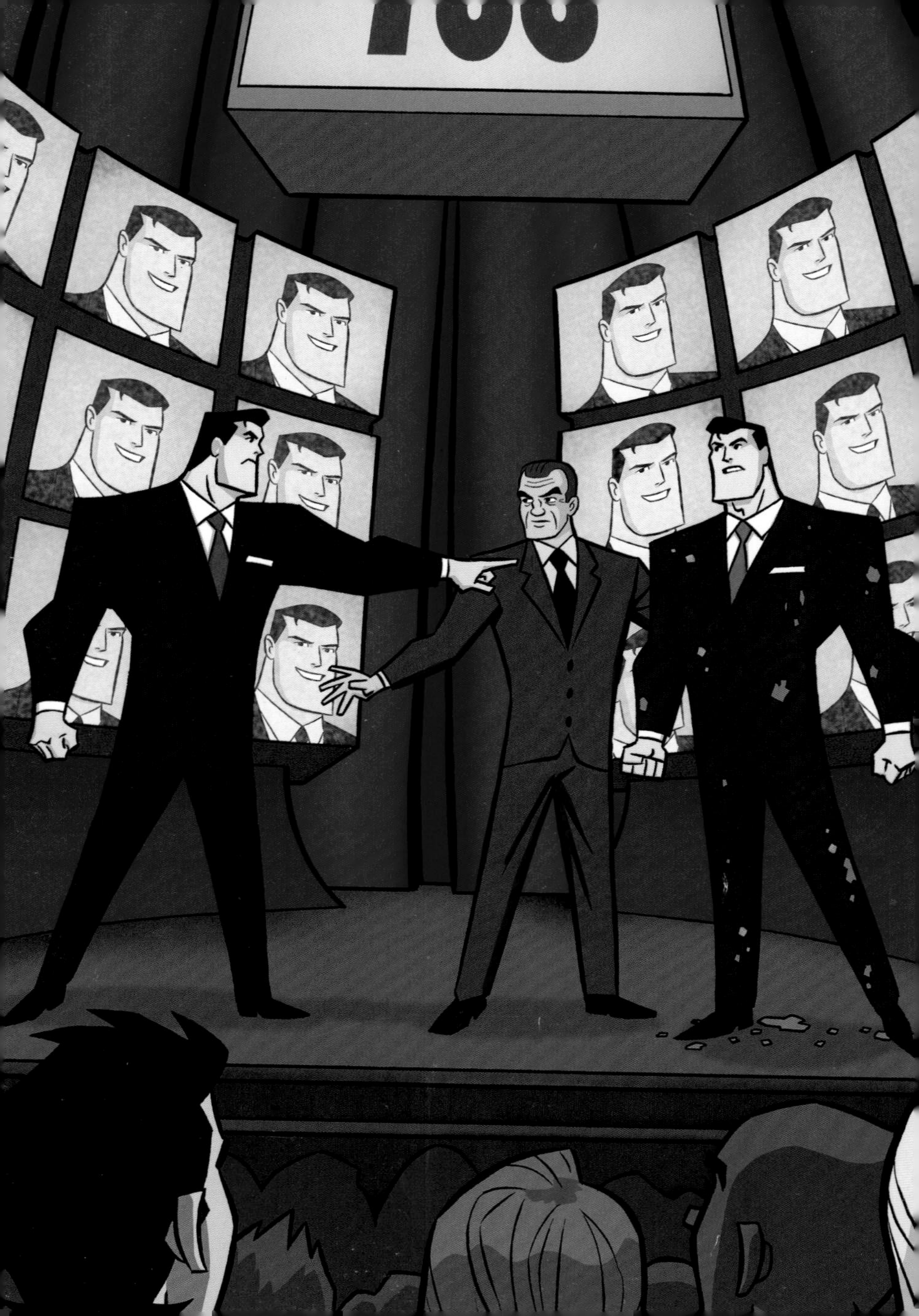

The impostor smiles evilly. "You want to know who I really am?" he asks. "I'll gladly show you the ugly truth behind Daggett's so-called beauty cream!"

Suddenly, the man's features transform from flesh and fabric to muddy, cruddy clay!

SQUELCH!

"IT'S CLAYFACE!" Daggett shouts in horror.

The menacing mud man grows several feet taller. His eyes glow yellow as he towers over the stage. Clayface shoots out hands of clay to grab Bruce Wayne and Roland Daggett. He picks them up and holds them high in the air as the crowd screams in panic.

"Looks like we're having ourselves one big, happy, dysfunctional family reunion!" Clayface says with a laugh.

Turn the page.

"What is the meaning of this?" Bruce asks. Out of the corner of his eye, he sees Tim running to the emergency exit.

"Roland Daggett and his poisonous product made me what I am today," Clayface snarls. "I've waited a long time to get my revenge."

The villain squeezes the men so hard they pass out. "Pretending to be Bruce Wayne was just a bonus," Clayface continues. "It gave me a nice fat paycheck from Daggett Industries. And now that I have both of you, I'll be getting an even fatter ransom. Ha, ha, ha!"

Bruce Wayne is trapped in the clutches of the malicious mud man. His only hope is that Robin, the Boy Wonder, will save the day ...

THE END

To follow another path, turn to page 16.

Bruce and Tim head to the outdoor garden. Zatanna's performance is taking place on a stage overlooking Gotham Harbor.

There is a direct view of the Lady Gotham statue. The statue is carrying a torch, and a pointed crown adorns her head.

The two friends arrive just in time to see Zatanna's last trick. Zatanna is wearing a fancy tuxedo and top hat.

"Ladies and gentlemen," she announces. "For my finale, I'll make Lady Gotham disappear!"

The audience buzzes with excitement.

Zatanna scans the crowd and sees Bruce's face. "First, I'll need a handsome volunteer to help me," she says, looking at the billionaire.

Turn the page.

But suddenly a nearby man dressed in a fine suit with slicked-back hair stands up. "I thought you'd never ask," he says. He pushes past Bruce and walks onto the stage.

"That's Roland Daggett," Bruce whispers to Tim. "Whenever he's around, trouble is sure to follow."

When Daggett gets on stage, Zatanna asks him to pull a velvet curtain across the platform. The curtain blocks the audience's view of Lady Gotham.

The Mistress of Magic waves her wand with a flourish and speaks her magic spell backwards.

"YdaL mahtoG, reappasid!"

POOF!

Zatanna gestures for Daggett to open the curtain. As he does so, the crowd gasps in amazement and erupts in applause.

Far out in the harbor, the statue of Lady Gotham is nowhere to be found!

"Told you she was amazing," Bruce says to Tim.

"You weren't kidding," the young man says, scratching his head.

They join in as the audience gives Zatanna a standing ovation. The Mistress of Magic smiles and takes a bow as admirers throw long-stemmed roses onto the stage.

But suddenly, the entire stage trembles and shakes.

RUUUMMBLE!

A large shape emerges from the water. It is the crowned head of Lady Gotham. The huge statue climbs onto the garden patio while the audience continues to applaud.

"Whoa!" Tim exclaims. "She IS amazing!"

Turn the page.

The living statue of Lady Gotham trudges toward Daggett. Its eyes are glowing, and it is dripping water and mud onto the stage.

Daggett staggers back and bumps into Zatanna. She is just as surprised as he is.

"Something tells me this isn't part of the show," Bruce says.

Lady Gotham grabs Daggett in her mighty grip and lifts him into the air. The oily businessman screams in fear. In a flash, the statue transforms into a large and menacing mud man.

"Is that any way to greet an old friend, Daggett?" the creature says.

"It's Clayface!" Bruce exclaims, as the crowd runs screaming for their lives.

If Bruce and Tim change into Batman and Robin, go to page 39.
If the two friends rush onto the stage to help, turn to page 63.

"We need to act fast," Bruce says. Let's get back to the car. "We need our suits." The daring duo race to the nearest exit, but it is blocked by the panicked crowd.

Meanwhile, Clayface commands the stage. "YOU made me the man I am today, Daggett! Your thugs drenched me in your poisonous product. Now I'm going to return the favor!"

Clayface leaps over the ledge with the crooked businessman in tow. The two fall into the muddy harbor.

SPLASH!!

Bruce and Tim run back to the edge of the dock and peer over the railing. The villain and his hostage are nowhere to be found.

"Looks like we'll need our scuba suits instead," Tim states.

"No, we're too late. It'll be impossible to track Clayface and Daggett now," Bruce says grimly, looking at the muddy water below.

THE END

To follow another path, turn to page 16.

As the crowd rushes closer to the stage, Bruce and Tim run toward the back exit. Bruce presses a button on his cufflink that alerts Alfred.

The two friends burst through the exit door to a secluded alley behind the arena. There they find a black town car with tinted windows pulling to a stop. Bruce and Tim enter the car and soon fly out of the sunroof as Batman and Robin!

WHOOSH!

Their grapnel guns hoist them to the roof of the building. At the top, the Dynamic Duo discover an open skylight located directly above the Auto Pavilion.

"I think it's time for us to make our dramatic entrance," Robin says.

The two caped heroes jump through the skylight to take on the fake Batman and help the Gray Ghost.

Turn the page.

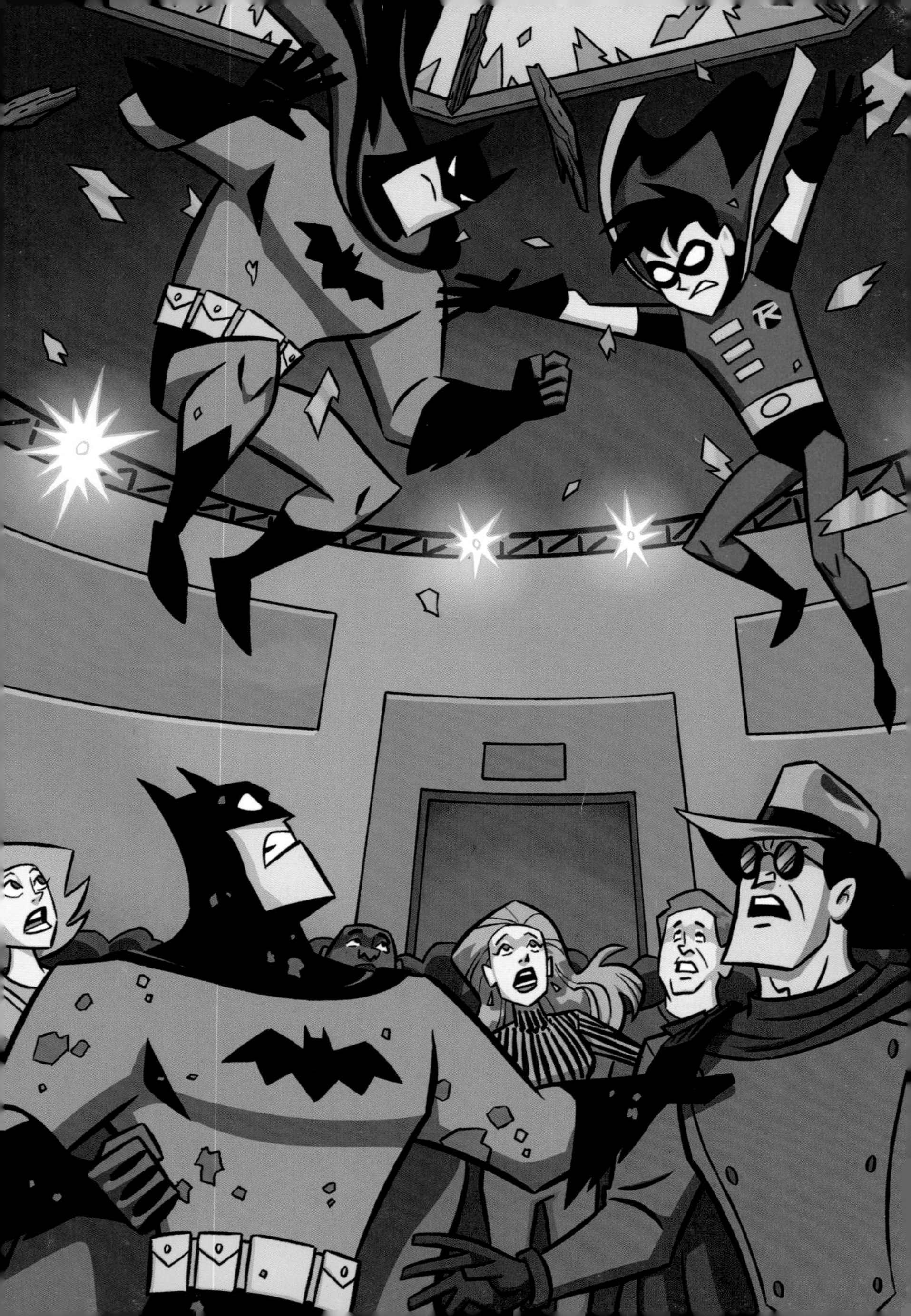

THUD! The Dynamic Duo lands on the stage.

"Show's over, Clayface!" Batman says.

"So, the World's Greatest Detective figured out my true identity," the fake Batman yells.

"You gave yourself away," Robin replies, pointing to the mud dripping around the villain's boots.

"That doesn't mean I'm giving myself up!" Clayface shouts.

He shifts back into his original form, and the crowd gasps in horror. Frightened, the Gray Ghost runs away from Clayface. The menacing mud man grows in size and towers over the stage. His eyes glow with rage.

"Not so fast, Mr. Ghost," shouts Clayface. "I'm your BIGGEST fan!"

Clayface stretches his arm across the stage and grabs the Gray Ghost. The beloved hero struggles in the villain's vice-like grip.

"You're a collector's item that's worth a lot of money!"

Batman and Robin race toward Clayface.
But the monster transforms his free arm into a
spiked mace and smashes the stage in half.

CRASH!

The heroes lose their balance and tumble
to the ground. Screaming with panic, the
crowd runs out of the pavilion. Clayface laughs
and trudges away with the Gray Ghost in his
clutches.

Thinking quickly, Batman throws several
sharp Batarangs at the fleeing foe. The weapons
slice through Clayface's arm. The hand holding
the actor drops to the ground and melts into a
puddle of mud.

PLOP!

Now free, the Gray Ghost runs to his car.

Clayface absorbs the puddle of mud back into
his body and regrows his limb. "Looks like I'll
have to deal with you first, Batman!" he bellows.
"Then I'll collect my ransom on Mr. Movie Star."

Turn the page.

Clayface tranforms his arms into two massive mallets and brings them down on Batman and Robin. But the Dynamic Duo rolls out of harm's way in the nick of time!

SMASH! SMASH!

"Did you know they were going to remake the Gray Ghost TV series?" Clayface asks as he continues his attack. "I was going to get the part. Then, thanks to Roland Daggett, Matt Hagen was lost forever. Now, there's only Clayface ... and he's MAD!"

The mud man pounds the ground again, spattering Batman and Robin with globs of clay.

Suddenly, an engine roars and tires squeal.

VROOOOM! SCREEECH!

"Quick, get in!" shouts a voice. It's the Gray Ghost in his famous car!

The heroes leap into the car and burn rubber. But Clayface turns himself into a wall of mud and blocks their path.

"Hang on to your capes!" Gray Ghost says. "I'm putting this baby on turbo!"

He presses the boost button, and the thrusters blast the car through the wall, spattering clay everywhere.

SPLOOSH!

"Nice moves," Batman says to his hero.

"Thanks, Batman," he says. "Like you, I do my own stunts."

Behind them, the muddy mess rapidly reforms itself into Clayface.

Turn the page.

The car rockets through the World's Fair like a silver bullet. Clayface fumes with anger.

"Looks like you found a new partner, Batman!" Clayface shouts. "So you won't be needing *this* one!" Clayface stretches his arm toward the speeding vehicle and plucks Robin out of his seat.

"Hey!" yelps the Boy Wonder.

"Robin!" Batman shouts.

The villain throws Robin to the ground and wraps him up in a cocoon of clay. The casing around the Boy Wonder quickly hardens, trapping him in an airtight shell.

The Gray Ghost slams on the brakes, causing the tires to squeal across the pavilion's polished floor.

SCREEEEEEE!

"Hang on!" he shouts at Batman. The experienced hero whips the car around and drives back to where Clayface is standing.

Batman leaps out of the moving vehicle and lunges at Clayface. He tackles the mudman to the ground. But Clayface moves fast. He quickly regains his feet and hurls Batman into a nearby wall.

SLAM!

"Ha!" Clayface cackles. "Back for an encore, Batman? I'll give you a repeat performance. Say goodbye to your new partner!"

The villain shoots a mud ball at the Gray Ghost.

WHOOSH!

But the Gray Ghost is ready. He uses his cape to deflect the muddy projectile.

"Bah! I won't be upstaged by this old has-been!" Clayface shouts. Then he melts into a puddle and slithers away toward the emergency exit.

Batman needs to act fast!

If Batman chases after Clayface, turn to page 48.
If Batman breaks Robin out of the cocoon, turn to page 74.

"If I let him out of my sight, there's no telling where he'll end up ... or who he'll end up becoming!" Batman tells the Gray Ghost. "You'll need to help free Robin."

The Caped Crusader hands a Batarang to the older hero and races after Clayface. He exits the World's Fair and follows a muddy trail down into the basement of the expo center.

"You've reached a dead end, Clayface," Batman says.

"Yes, it's your dead end, Batman!" Clayface replies, leaping from the shadows. Clayface transforms his fist into a spiked mace and swings it at the Dark Knight.

SWOOSH!

Batman backflips out of harm's way seconds before the weapon smashes the floor beneath him.

CRASH!

Thinking quickly, Batman produces another Batarang from his Utility Belt. He throws it with expert accuracy at the fuse box across the room. The razor-sharp weapon easily cuts through the electrical wires.

ZZARK!

The room instantly plunges into complete darkness. Batman presses a switch in his Utility Belt. Infrared lenses drop over his eyes inside his cowl. He switches on the night-vision.

Batman watches as Clayface crashes around blindly in the dark. The hero must act fast before the villain causes any more destruction.

Batman nimbly rolls under Clayface's swinging arms and comes up near the mud man's midsection. He inserts an electrically charged Batarang between the villain's folds of clay and leaps to safety.

Turn the page.

Just then, the Gray Ghost arrives, and the Dark Knight pulls him to the ground. He covers the man with his protective cape right before —

ZZZAAAARK!

The high-voltage weapon electrocutes Clayface! The mudman shakes and shutters, sending clay and mud spattering everywhere!

Seconds later, the generator comes on, lighting up the basement. Batman stands up and helps Gray Ghost to his feet. He looks over at Clayface who is laying face down on the ground.

"Is he dead?" he asks.

"You can't really kill Clayface," Batman replies. "He's very unpredictable like that."

Suddenly the different piles of living mud pull themselves together into one big mound. Clayface rises taller and angrier than before.

"You're so smart, Batman!" laughs the villain. "I wish I could be just like you!"

Clayface morphs into Batman. The two opponents are now identical. The Gray Ghost can't tell them apart!

One Batman punches the other into the wall.

BAM!

"Why are you hitting yourself?" he cackles.

The Gray Ghost wants to help but can't tell which is the real Batman. Suddenly he has an idea and rushes to a nearby fire hose.

Batman recovers and tackles his twin terror, wrestling him to the ground. He lands a few jabs on the impostor's jaw, but it feels like he's punching granite.

POW! WHAP!

Turn the page.

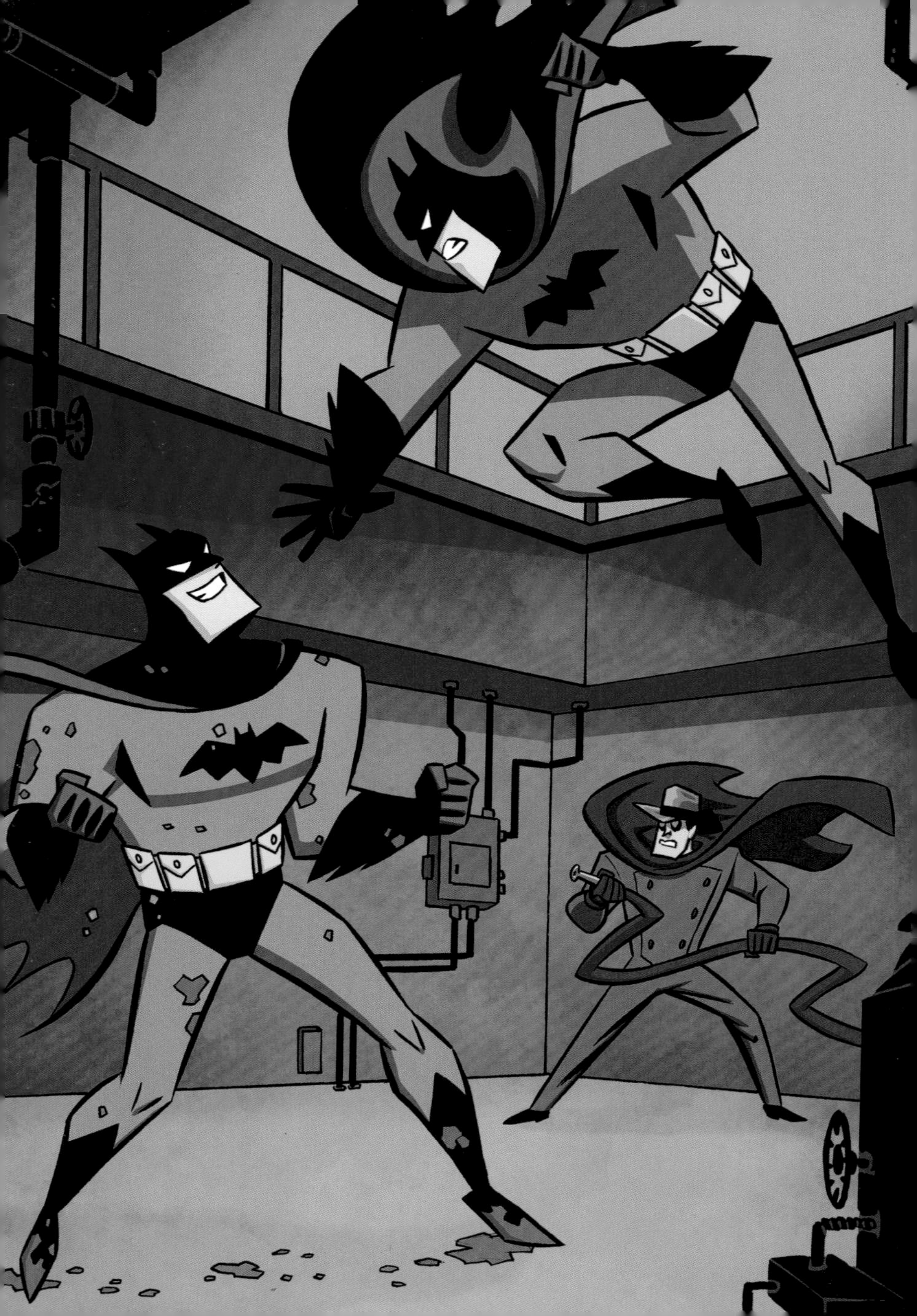

The fighting foes continue their struggle. They are a tangle of capes, masks, gloves, and boots. The Gray Ghost is just as confused as he was before.

"Sorry, Batman," he says. "This is for your own good!" The Gray Ghost turns on the hose.

WHOOOOSH!

The powerful spray of water knocks the two fighters off their feet. They both tumble down the hall and land flat on their backs.

WHUMP!

Each of them is soaked, but only one has clay seeping through his suit.

"Looks like I've flushed you out, Clayface!" the Gray Ghost says.

He advances toward the villain, keeping the powerful stream of water steady.

Turn the page.

"I'm melting!!" Clayface screams as he shifts back into his original form.

"AAAAAAAGH!"

The continuous blast of water dissolves the villain into a puddle of mud that slowly drips down a nearby sewer drain.

"It'll be a long time before Clayface pulls himself together again," Batman says. "Thank you for your help."

The two men shake hands.

"I was returning the favor," Gray Ghost replies. "When it comes to hero work, one hand must wash the other!"

THE END

To follow another path, turn to page 16.

Bruce and Tim rush toward the nearest exit. The billionaire presses a secret button in his cufflink that activates the Batmobile via remote control.

"That guy up there sure looks like you," Tim says.

"I'm not impressed," Bruce scoffs. "If Daggett hired some look-alike to sell his product with my image, he's reached a new low."

The duo leave the World's Fair. They run a few blocks and turn the corner into a dark, secluded alley. Minutes later, the Batmobile pulls up.

VROOOM!

Bruce and Tim enter the vehicle and shut the doors. They quickly change into Batman and Robin. Then Batman drives back to the World's Fair.

Turn the page.

The sleek and armored Batmobile gains a lot of attention from the crowd outside. There are cheers and applause as the Dynamic Duo emerge.

Batman and Robin sprint past the on-lookers and head for the *ReNuYu Too* booth. When they arrive, the stage is swarmed by rows of people. Roland Daggett and the Bruce Wayne impostor are throwing free samples of the cream into the crowd.

"This is just a small taste of eternal youth," Daggett says.

SWISH! The Dynamic Duo swing over the crowd on their Batropes. They land on the stage, surprising the two men.

Daggett quickly responds. "If anyone is in desperate need of my product, it's Batman!" shouts Daggett. "All that crime-fighting has taken its toll. He looks like he's 75 years old!"

Batman pushes past Daggett to confront the impostor. "Who are you?" he demands.

The man takes a few steps back, leaving a trail of mud between him and the Caped Crusader.

"I'm Bruce Wayne," he says. "And if you want an autograph, you'll have to stand in line like everybody else."

"Nice try," Batman says, looking at the trail of mud. "But you gave yourself away—Clayface!"

Suddenly the man pretending to be Bruce Wayne shoves Batman to the floor. He rips through his clothes and transforms into the large monster made of living clay.

"AAARRR!"

Turn the page.

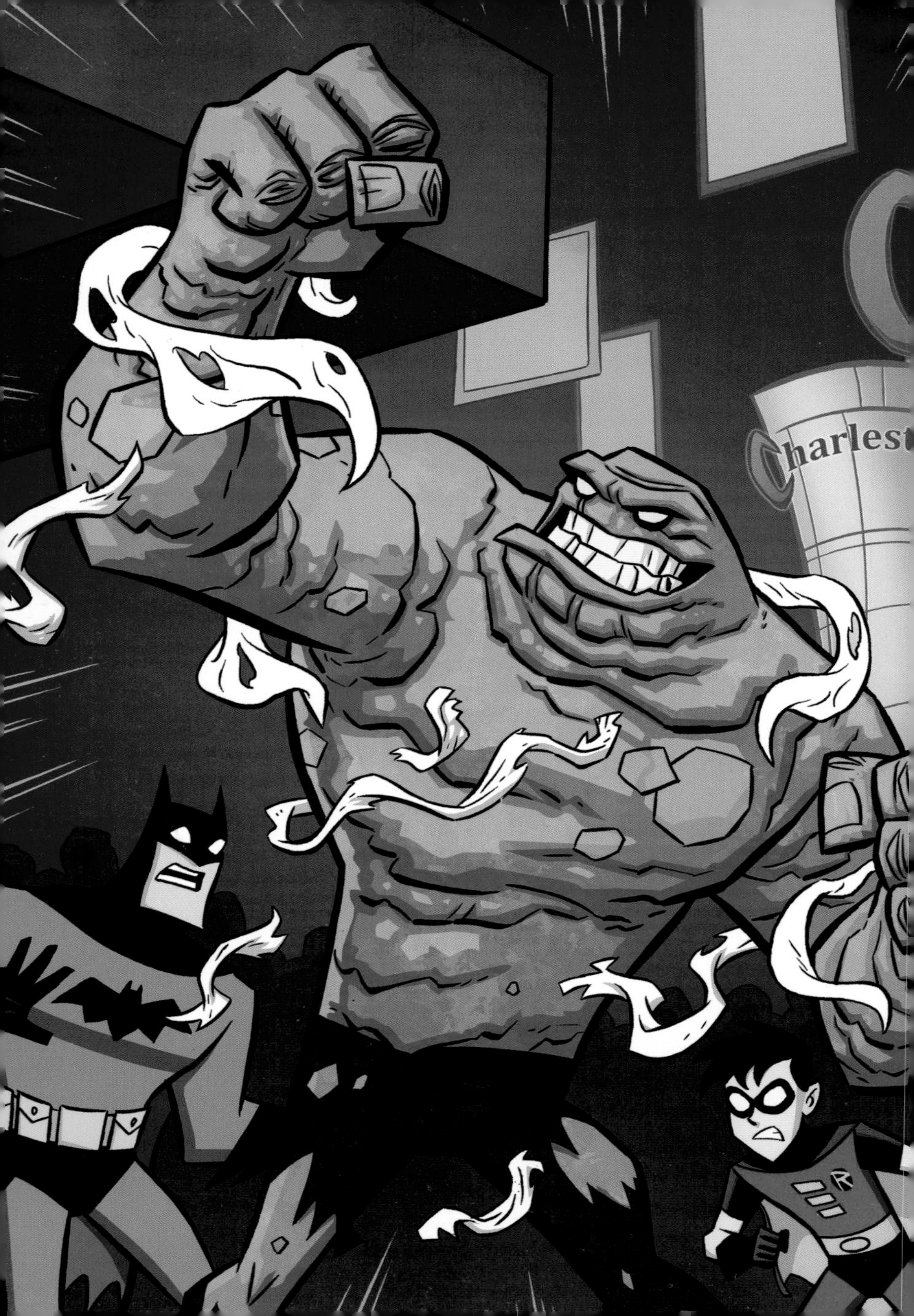
harlest

"What is the meaning of this?" Daggett hollers.

"Posing as Bruce Wayne was just icing on the cake," Clayface says. "It allowed me to get close enough to do this ..."

Clayface's muddy arm extends across the stage. He grabs Daggett and lifts him into the air.

"Your poisonous product made me like this," Clayface snarls. "I've waited a long time to claim my sweet revenge."

The creature squeezes the slimy businessman in his grasp. Daggett grunts in pain.

Batman jumps to his feet, ready for action.

If Batman and Robin try to defeat Clayface on stage, turn to page 60.

If they lure Clayface away from the crowd, turn to page 91.

"We need to end this fast," Batman says to Robin.

"Let's give Daggett a hand," the Boy Wonder quips.

Both heroes pull out their razor-sharp Batarangs and hurl them with expert accuracy at Clayface.

ZIP! ZIP!

Each bladed weapon slices through the mud man's arms, severing them from his body!

The arms holding Daggett drop to the floor and dissolve into a puddle of wet clay. Daggett scrambles to his feet as the mound of mud slithers back toward its owner.

With Clayface momentarily distracted, Batman and Robin attack! They team up against the monster, delivering a double whammy of punches and kicks.

WHAP! POW!

Clayface stumbles backward. The display cases topple, scattering bottles of face cream everywhere.

SMASH!

Dollops of cream spatter across the stage and onto the crowd.

As Clayface falls over the edge of the stage, he shoots two globs of clay from his fists at Batman and Robin. But the Dynamic Duo drop to the ground. The projectiles whiz over them ... and hit Daggett instead!

SPLORCH!

The disgraced businessman curses his luck.

Batman and Robin leap off the stage in pursuit of Clayface, but they're too late. Clayface is gone!

Turn the page.

Clayface is nowhere to be found. All the heroes find is a puddle of mud and some dirty footprints. Batman scoops up a sample of the mud with a vial from his Utility Belt.

"We need to track down Clayface and clean up this mess," he says.

Robin grimly scans the crowd again. "I don't know, Batman," the sidekick replies. "Clayface can become anybody. Right now, I'm afraid he has us stumped!"

THE END

To follow another path, turn to page 16.

Clayface waves Daggett around in the air like a ragdoll.

"I've waited a long time to get my revenge!" Clayface growls. "And here you are, playing the part of a respectable and reformed man ... while *I'm* seen as the monster! That's an illusion worthy of Zatanna herself!"

"Let me go!" Daggett pleads. "I'll pay anything!"

Bruce and Tim rush onto the stage. "Clayface!" Bruce shouts. "There's no need to harm anyone!"

"You stay out of this, pretty boy!" Clayface yells. He hurls a mud ball at Bruce, knocking him flat on his back.

SPLAT!

"Always thrill-seeking," Zatanna says, helping Bruce to his feet. "You haven't changed a bit."

"That's it!" he says. "We can certainly use a change. Think you can work your magic?"

"Follow me," Zatanna says. "We need to work fast."

Turn the page.

The Mistress of Magic guides Bruce and Tim through a trap door under the stage. Several of her magic show props are stored here, including the Transformation Chamber. It is a large ornate box with carvings of Egyptian hieroglyphs.

"Get in!" Zatanna says, and the duo complies. She waves her magic wand and says the magic words, *"Egnahc otni namtaB dna niboR!"*

POOF!

The chamber door opens in a puff of smoke to reveal Batman and Robin inside!

"Thank you, old friend," Batman says. "It's time to put an end to Clayface's criminal act!"

The Dynamic Duo pull out their grapnel guns and aim them at the light structures at the top of the stage. Batman holds Zatanna as they prepare to launch into action.

CHOOM!

Two high-tension wires coil around a metal girder. The trio is hoisted up through the trap door and land in front of Clayface and Daggett.

"Show's over!" cries Robin.

"Hardly, Boy Blunder!" Clayface spits. "You're just in time for my grand finale. Let's find out if this little jailbird can fly! HA HA HA!"

Clayface morphs into a giant baseball player in complete uniform. He winds up a pitch and throws Daggett over the edge toward the harbor below!

"AAAAAAH!"

If Batman and Robin try to trap Clayface, turn to page 66.
If the Dynamic Duo rush to save Daggett, turn to page 87.

Daggett plummets to the water below. Then there is silence.

Batman and Robin act fast. If they can trounce Clayface quickly, they might be able to fish Daggett out of the harbor before it's too late.

"HA!" Clayface laughs. "This is a one-man show, so I'm giving you the axe!" The mud man morphs his arm into a giant axe and slices it through the air.

The heroes dodge the sharp blade as it buries itself deep into the stage floor.

CHOP!!

Clayface pulls out the blade and swings again. The Dynamic Duo quickly duck under the huge axe as the blade sinks into a nearby wall.

CHOP!

"Phew!" Robin cries. "That was a close shave!"

Turn the page.

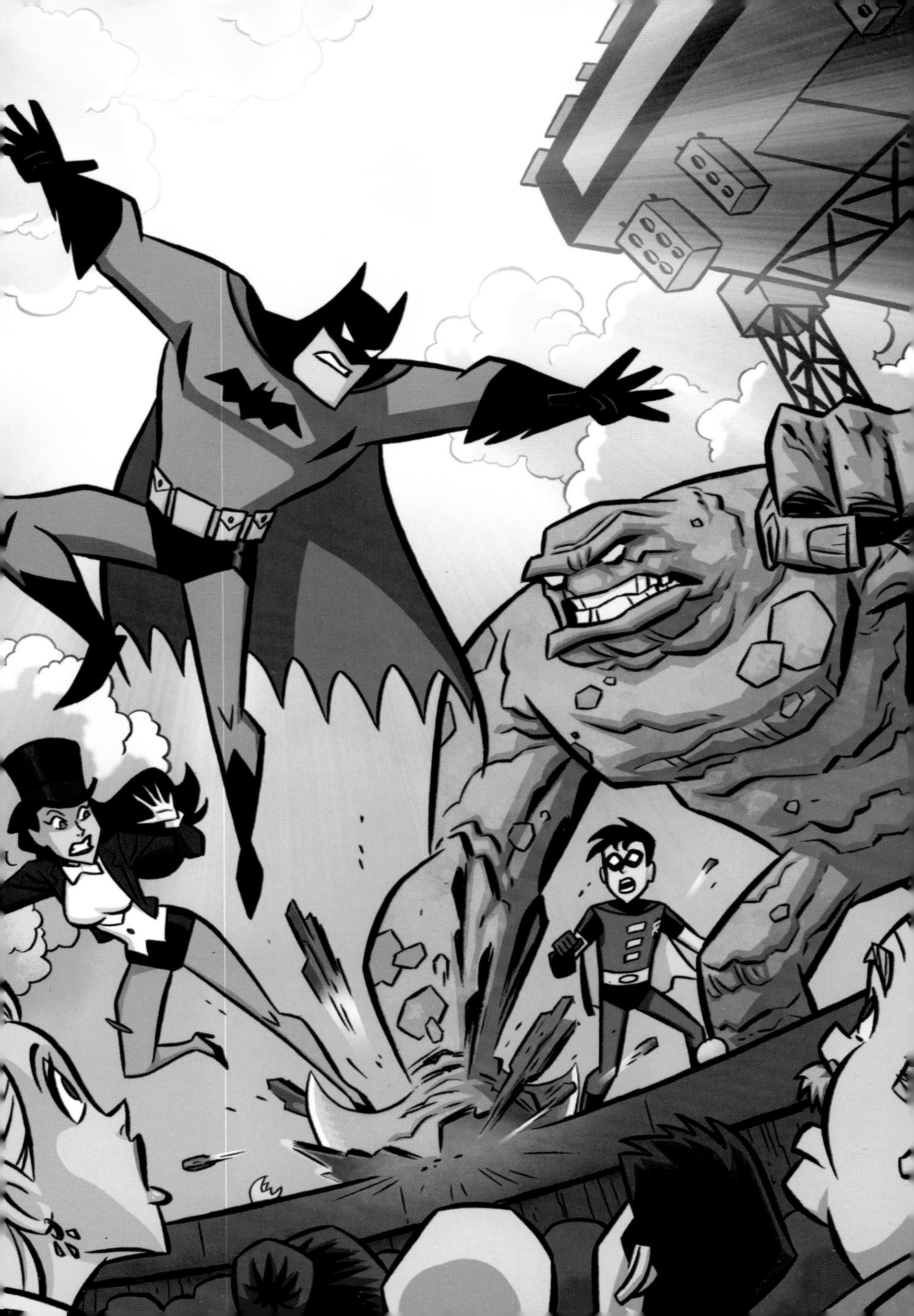

As Batman and Robin battle Clayface, Zatanna runs to the edge of the deck and looks over. Daggett is dangling from a scraggly rock, holding on for dear life.

"Hang in there," Zatanna shouts.

She taps her wand against the railing and says, "*Dnaw ot epor!*" The wand transforms into a rope. The Mistress of Magic ties one end to the railing and lowers the other end down to Daggett.

Zatanna lets the businessman pull himself up as she races back to aid the Dynamic Duo.

"Hold still, will ya?!" Clayface snarls as he pulls his axe-hand free and smashes it through the stage once more.

With Clayface's axe stuck in the floor, Batman and Robin see their chance. They both charge at the villain and slam into him with a double kick to the chest.

WHAM!

The creature stumbles backward. Then the heroes follow up their attack with a jab-and-hook two-hit combo.

WHAP! WHAP!

But this time their punches barely faze the mud man.

"Who's next for a dirt nap?" Clayface taunts. "The bat or the brat?" He grabs both Batman and Robin in his massive fists and raises them high in the air. "How about a two-for-one special?"

Before he can hurl the Dynamic Duo into the harbor, Zatanna blocks his path. *"Part rood, nepo!"* she commands.

The trap door beneath Clayface opens, and the villain falls through the tight space. His clay arms break off against the edges, leaving Batman and Robin on the stage in two puddles of mud.

SPLORT! SPLASH!

The mud puddles then slither away from the heroes and down the hole.

Turn the page.

"Thanks for lending a hand," Batman says to Zatanna.

"Anytime," she replies with a bow.

Daggett walks over and peers into the darkness. "Good riddance," he spits.

"Let this be a warning to you, sir," Robin says. "Your past will always come back to haunt you."

Suddenly an enormous hulking brute bursts through the stage floor.

SMASH!

"BOO!" shouts Clayface. He blasts Daggett with two blobs of clay, pinning his feet to the ground. The sticky compound hardens quickly.

"One way or another, you'll be sleeping with the fishes tonight, Daggett," the villain says, as Daggett struggles to break free. "These cement shoes ought to do the trick!"

Zatanna waves her magic wand and is about to cast a spell, but Clayface covers her mouth with clay.

SPLAT!

"No more tricks out of you!" he says.

Batman and Robin lunge at Clayface. But he swats them away like insects. Then he trudges toward Daggett, intending to throw him into the harbor once again.

Batman pries the clay off Zatanna's mouth and the magician yells, *"TteggaD, raeppasid!"*

POOF!

Daggett disappears just as Clayface reaches for him. The mad villain falls face first onto the ground.

Turn the page.

"Consider that your last performance, Clayface," Batman says. "It's lights out for you!"

The Dark Knight shoots his grapnel gun at the overhead lights and snares the support beam holding them in place. Then he rips the oversized lights down with all his might.

The lights crash down on Clayface, zapping the monster with a high-voltage electric current!

ZZZZAAARRRRK!

Clayface shrinks back to his normal size and stumbles around dazed. "Let it never be said that Matt Hagen failed to bring down the house!" he says, and crumples into a smoldering heap.

The heroes breathe a sigh of relief. "Where's Daggett?" Batman asks Zatanna.

The Mistress of Magic smiles. "Oh, he's doing some sight-seeing," she says, pointing out at Gotham Harbor.

Batman and Robin turn to see that the missing statue of Lady Gotham has reappeared. Standing at a window inside her crown is Roland Daggett!

"Let me out of here!" he yells out into the open water.

"That was quite the finale, huh?" Robin says. "What are we going to do about Clayface?"

"We'll need to take him to Arkham Asylum for therapy," says Batman. "I'll call Commissioner Gordon now."

"I have an airtight casket you can put him in until the authorities arrive," Zatanna offers.

"That would be perfect," Batman replies. "He can make his grand entrance at Arkham Asylum the way he would have wanted … with style!"

THE END

To follow another path, turn to page 16.

Batman rushes over to Robin. He scans the area, but Clayface is nowhere to be found.

Working quickly, the Dark Knight reaches into his Utility Belt and retrieves a laser cutter. It shoots a red-hot beam that slices through the clay cocoon's tough exterior until it cracks open.

SSSSSSKRACK!

The Gray Ghost parks his car and runs over to help Batman. Both heroes tear away chunks of clay. Finally, Robin is free … but he's barely breathing. The Dark Knight lifts his partner's limp form in his arms.

"Batman, is there anything I can do to help?" the Gray Ghost asks.

"Yes," Batman replies. "Let me use your car."

"Of course," says the Gray Ghost. "It's all yours."

The Caped Crusader buckles Robin into the passenger seat of the Gray Ghost's famous car. Then he climbs into the driver's seat and revs the engine.

"Thank you, old friend," Batman says. The Gray Ghost tips his hat, and the Dynamic Duo speed out of the World's Fair toward the outskirts of Gotham City.

Batman touches his earpiece to communicate with the Batcave.

DEET DEET DEET

"Sir?" Alfred's voice crackles over the speaker.

"Prep a table," Batman says. "Robin needs medical attention. He's been in prolonged contact with Clayface's chemical compound. We need to flush out his system."

"My word!" Alfred exclaims. "Consider it done, sir."

CLICK.

The line disconnects and the car completes the rest of the journey in stony silence.

Turn the page.

Minutes later, the rocket-like vehicle streaks into the Batcave.

Batman carries Robin to the Batcave's sickroom. Alfred is prepped and ready. He places an oxygen mask on Robin's face.

"He'll be alright, Master Bruce," he says, comforting the Caped Crusader.

The loyal butler swabs Robin's arm and prepares to inject fluids with a syringe. Suddenly, Robin lunges from the table, knocking Batman and Alfred to the ground.

"AAAAAH!" he screams. "I hate needles!"

Then in the blink of an eye, the Boy Wonder transforms into Clayface!

"Surprise!" shouts the shape-shifter.

"Well, dust my dustpan!" Alfred exclaims and rushes out of the Batcave.

"Where's Robin?" Batman demands.

"HA!" Clayface laughs. "I pulled the old bait-and-switch back at the fair, see? But don't worry, I've got plenty of clay to go around!"

Clayface extends his arms and blasts two mud balls at Batman. But the Dark Knight backflips over the operating table and uses it to deflect the blast. *SPLAT! SPLAT!*

Clayface then transforms his arms into twin mallets and prepares to strike. Batman shoves the table at the clay creature with full force— cutting him in half!

SPLORCH!

"Look at me!" the top part of Clayface laughs. "I'm beside myself!"

The mud man quickly becomes whole again and lunges at Batman. However, the Caped Crusader is ready. He somersaults forward, jump-kicking Clayface square in the chest.

WHAM!

Clayface stumbles backward and topples over the ledge. He plummets down into the Batcave's trophy room!

Turn the page.

Dazed and disoriented, Clayface rises to his feet. He is surrounded by rows of dimly lit glass display cases. Each case contains lethal weapons that belonged to Batman's greatest enemies.

"Whoa!" Clayface exclaims. "Looks like you're taking too much of your work home with you, Batman." The villain trudges along the display cases, admiring the Caped Crusader's collection.

Batman follows Clayface to the trophy room. "Surrender and I'll go easy on you," Batman says.

"Are you kidding?" Clayface scoffs. "I've hit the jackpot! Look at all these souvenirs! I bet I could fetch a good price for them on the black market!"

Batman springs into action just as Clayface smashes the nearest glass case and pulls out the huge Joker Mallet!

Clayface transforms himself into the Joker. He's the spitting image of the Clown Prince of Crime!

"Batter up, Batman!" the villain cackles.

Turn the page.

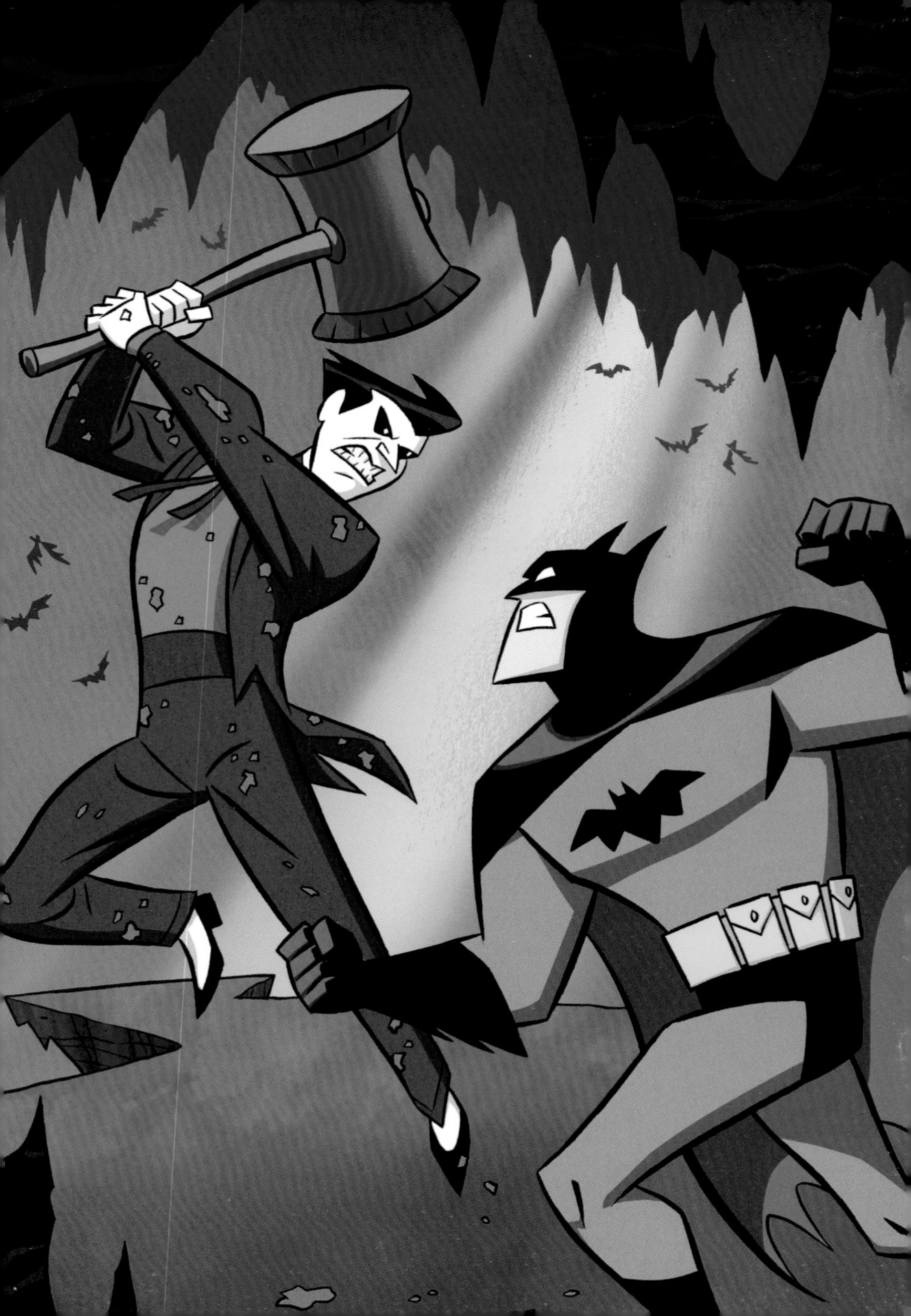

The imitation Joker takes a swing from the left, but Batman dodges the attack.

"Is that the best you've got?" Batman asks.

The cackling villain takes another swing from the right, and Batman ducks.

"I'm sure you can do better than that," Batman taunts.

Gritting his teeth in anger, the Joker impostor swings one last time and brings the heavy mallet down on Batman.

WHOOSH!

Quickly, Batman grabs the handle of the mallet. He uses the villain's momentum to hurl him over his shoulder.

"That's strike three," growls the Dark Knight. "You're out of here!"

The fake Joker sails through the air and crashes into another display case.

SMASH!

If Batman keeps fighting Clayface in the trophy room, go to page 81.

If Batman drags the villain away from the weapons, turn to page 101.

The phony Joker is sprawled in the ruins of the display case. Shards of glass lay all around him. Reeling from the impact, the shape-shifter reverts back to his original form.

Suddenly, the weapon in the display tumbles out and lands on Clayface's head. **CLUNK!**

It is a long, solid gold cane. Its handle is shaped like a question mark. Clayface's eyes light up as he grips the weapon. In a flash, Clayface transforms into the Riddler—the infernal Prince of Puzzles!

He presses a button on the tip and a spray of poison gas shoots out. **FSSSSSSS!**

Batman covers his mouth and whirls his cape around to blow away the toxic cloud. In a flash, the Dark Knight delivers a roundhouse kick. It knocks the Riddler's cane out of the villain's hand.

CRACK!

Turn the page.

"Here's a riddle, Batman!" the fake Riddler shouts. "When is a man drowned, but still not wet?" The Riddler's arms shift into jets of exploding mud, blasting Batman into another display case.

SPLLOOOORRRCH!

"When he's drowning in quicksand!" Clayface cries. "*HAHAHA!*"

The geysers bury the Caped Crusader under an immovable mountain of mud.

All is still, except for Clayface's cackling laughter. Suddenly, the mound of mud shifts. A black-gloved fist punches its way out.

POW!

Another fist follows, and Batman digs his way out. He spits dirt and scans for Clayface. The shape-shifter has disappeared again.

Just then a sleek, black-clad figure slinks into view and a long leather whip cracks at Batman's feet.

SNAP!

Catwoman steps out of the shadows, wielding her infamous whip.

"What's the matter, Batman?" Catwoman asks. "Cat got your tongue?" She lashes out, striking the whip at Batman once again.

CRACK!

The Dark Knight nimbly sidesteps the attack, and grips the whip in his fist. Then he yanks hard, spinning his foe round in circles until she's wrapped up in her own whip.

"You can't keep this cat tied down," hisses the bogus Catwoman. She dissolves into liquid clay and slithers through the coils of the whip.

The mud slides across the room and reforms as Clayface. He smashes his fist into another display case.

SMASH!

Turn the page.

More of the Joker's deadly party gags spill out onto the floor. Clayface once again transforms into the Joker.

"Where does that clown get all his incredible toys?" he asks.

The villain picks up a deck of razor sharp playing cards and throws them at the Dark Knight. "Pick a card, Batman, any card!" he shouts with glee. "The Jokers are wild! Ah, ha, ha!"

Batman drops to the ground as the cards whiz overhead like darts.

SHUNK! SHUNK! SHUNK!

They embed themselves in the cavern wall, inches away from their target. Cursing his luck, the wild-eyed Joker picks up a rubber chicken and whoopee cushion.

While he tries to figure out what they do, Batman spots a small metal object amongst the broken glass. Stealthily, he rolls forward and swipes it up from the ground.

"It's my turn to deal," Batman says.

Batman grabs the Joker's hand … and gives him a shocking surprise!

ZZZZZZZARK!

A high-voltage electric current courses through the villain.

"**AAAAARGH!**" he cries. The Joker's face melts away and Clayface transforms back into a mud man.

"That's all, folks," he mumbles and falls forward into a smoking heap.

Batman opens his palm to reveal a concealed Joker Buzzer! The tiny trinket zapped Clayface into unconsciousness.

"Looks like the joke is on you," the hero says.

Turn the page.

Alfred comes out of hiding and joins Batman in the trophy room. "My word!" he exclaims, observing the damage. The once pristine and organized gallery is now in shambles. The keepsakes from Batman's crime-fighting cases lay scattered about in a mixture of glass and dirt.

Just then Batman receives a message on his communicator. It's from Robin! The Boy Wonder is alive and well back at the World's Fair.

"I'll be right there," Batman says.

"Good," says the Boy Wonder. "Because the Gray Ghost wants his car back!" Batman smiles.

Alfred regards the motionless form of Clayface on the ground and wrinkles his nose.

"What about him, sir? Is he to become part of your collection as well?"

"No, thank you, Alfred," Batman replies. "I think the best place for Clayface to be observed is at Arkham Asylum!"

THE END

To follow another path, turn to page 16.

In a flash, Batman and Robin rush to the edge of the deck overlooking the harbor. Daggett is plummeting to the water below. They shoot their grappling guns at the falling man.

SHOOM! SHOOM!

Two strong cables circle around Daggett's ankles and abruptly stop his descent.

"Hey!" Daggett complains. "You're wrinkling my new suit!"

"Oh, yeah, and I'm sure the river would have done wonders for it!" Robin yells down to him.

Robin looks at Batman and shakes his head. "You'd think he'd be grateful for us saving his life," the Boy Wonder adds.

The Dynamic Duo loop their gadgets around the railing and tie them tight. Then they begin pulling Daggett back up.

"Hurry up!" Daggett whines.

Turn the page.

As Batman and Robin save Daggett, Clayface turns into a puddle of mud and slithers up behind them. Then he reforms himself and pushes the Dynamic Duo over the railing!

"It's a great day for a dip!" he cries.

Batman and Robin fall past Daggett toward the cold water below. Thinking quickly, Batman reaches out and grabs a jagged rock with his right hand. He stops his fall and slams into the rock face.

WHAM!

Using his lightning-fast reflexes, the Dark Knight grabs Robin with his left hand in the nick of time. "Nice catch!" says the Boy Wonder. "Thanks."

Clayface pounds his fist in anger.

The monstrous mud man starts punching the rock face under the railing and loosens big chunks of stone. A boulder comes tumbling down directly toward the Dynamic Duo!

"I should have been a musician," Clayface cackles. "I can really rock!"

Zatanna rushes to the rescue. She waves her wand and speaks a spell, *"Skcor ot srehtaef!"* Instantly, the avalanche of rocks transforms into a cloud of fluffy feathers that flutter harmlessly through the air.

Clayface whirls around to face Zatanna. The magician points her wand at him.

"Don't move or I'll use it on you too!" she shouts. The mud man gulps and puts his hands in the air.

"You're not the only one who can pull off a disappearing act," Clayface replies. He dissolves into a lumpy pile of mud and slithers down the side of the dock.

Zatanna watches the clump of living clay plunge into the harbor below.

SPLASH!

Turn the page.

The magician runs over to the railing. "Hang on!" she yells at the heroes. "I've got something up my sleeve!"

Zatanna pulls out a colorful scarf that is several feet long and lowers it over the side. Robin clutches it and Zatanna pulls him up. Batman then effortlessly scales up the rocky surface.

"Thanks for lending a hand," Batman says.

"I always come prepared when I do a show in Gotham," she replies. "You never know what kind of surprises will rear their ugly heads."

"Speaking of ugly heads, where's Clayface?" Robin asks.

"He escaped into the harbor," Batman replies. "But we'll be ready when he resurfaces. In the meantime, we still have an oily fish on our hooks to reel in."

The Dynamic Duo drag the grumpy Daggett onto the dock as the sun sets in the distance.

THE END

To follow another path, turn to page 16.

Batman throws exploding gas pellets at the monstrous mud man.

PAF! PAF! PAF!

Clayface hacks and coughs as he drops Daggett. "Oof!" grunts the disgruntled businessman.

Batman flings his Batrope around Daggett's leg and yanks him away from his captor.

"You want Daggett?" Batman asks. "Come and get him."

The Dark Knight heaves Daggett over his shoulder and jumps off the stage.

"Make way, coming through!" Robin yells, clearing a path toward the exit.

Turn the page.

Batman races out of the arena and heads toward the Batmobile.

"Robin, buy us some time!" he says as Clayface barrels down the hall directly at them.

The Boy Wonder pulls out his collapsible bo staff and straightens it. He then slides it through the door handles, jamming them in place to delay Clayface for a few moments.

The mud man pounds on the doors with his fists.

BOOM! BOOM! BOOM!

Pressing a button on his Utility Belt, Batman commands the Batmobile's doors to slide open. He puts Daggett on the passenger seat.

"Don't ... touch ... anything," Batman growls. "The armored plating will keep you safe from Clayface, but not from me."

SMASH! CRASH!

Clayface continues to pound on the door and then abruptly stops.

"It's quiet," Robin states warily.

"Too quiet," observes Batman. "Clayface likes to put on a show. He doesn't shy away from making a grand entrance."

As if on cue, the doors start to vibrate. Mud seeps through the cracks and crevices around them. Streams of thick liquid dirt ooze under the door to puddle around Batman and Robin.

"Ew, gross!" Robin exclaims.

"Get back!" Batman commands.

The Dynamic Duo tumble away from the doors as the puddles of living clay reform into Clayface.

"It's showtime!" he announces.

Turn the page.

Batman and Robin fling their Batarangs at the menacing mud man. But Clayface just absorbs them into his body.

"Hahaha!" he laughs. "That tickles! Now it's my turn. Fetch!" Clayface spews the weapons back at the heroes.

FWIP! FWIP!

The Dynamic Duo ducks for cover as the sharp weapons sail overhead.

Clayface rushes past the heroes and leaps onto the Batmobile. He pounds the roof with his fists. "Knock, knock, Daggett!"

The Batmobile's exterior shows no sign of damage. Clayface is furious. He transforms his arm into the sharp spinning blade of a buzzsaw!

"I'm going to rip open this tin can and pull you out like a sardine!"

BZZZZZZZZ!

Turn the page.

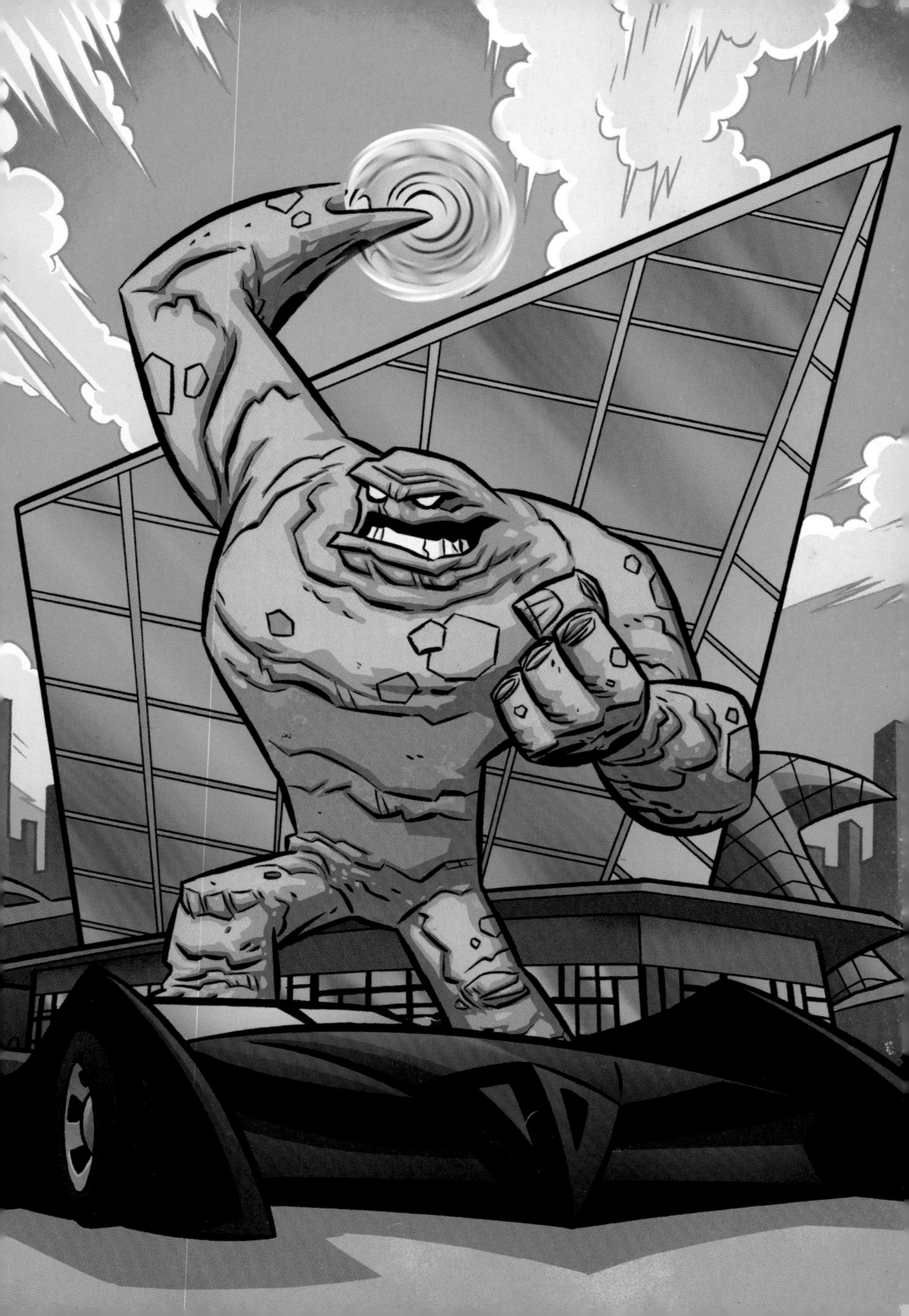

Clayface slices at the Batmobile's roof.

"How about I trim a little off the top?" Clayface laughs.

Sparks fly into the air as metal scrapes against metal.

SKRREEEECH! The buzzsaw scratches the armor but can't cut through.

"Hey, Creature Feature! Watch the paint job!" Robin shouts. The Boy Wonder hurls a Batarang at Clayface. But the weapon gets swallowed up inside the villain's muddy form.

"Bah, that tickles!" Clayface cackles. "Besides, kids like you should be seen and not heard!"

The mudman blasts a mud ball at Robin, hitting him right in the face.

SPLAT!

Batman rushes to his partner's side. "Hold still, Robin. I'll get that off in no time," he says as he peels off the clay.

"I'm just getting warmed up!" Clayface yells.

He shoots another mud ball, but the Dynamic Duo spring into action. They leap onto the Batmobile and tackle the mad villain.

WHUMP! THUD.

The three of them roll onto the hood of the vehicle. Robin has Clayface in a headlock while Batman pins down his legs.

"Bah! You think your fancy moves can hold me? I've got some smooth moves of my own!"

Clayface dissolves his body and melts through the grasp of his opponents. Then he slithers back onto the roof of the Batmobile and reforms himself bigger than before.

"Ha! Looks like I gave you the slip again!" Clayface bellows. "Your time is up!" He morphs his fists into massive mallets and raises them high.

"Time to kick things up a notch," Robin says.

"Good idea," Batman agrees.

Turn the page.

With lightning-fast reflexes, the Dynamic Duo unleash jump kicks to Clayface's midsection.

WHAP! WHAP!

"OOF!"

Clayface is knocked off balance and rolls off the back end of the Batmobile. He lands hard on the pavement, splattering wet mud all around. The monstrous mud man rises to his feet, his eyes glowing with rage.

"Now we're warmed up and bringing the heat!" Robin says.

Batman presses another small button on his Utility Belt. The Batmobile roars to life!

VROOOOM!

The Batmobile's tailpipe belches a fireball— directly at Clayface!

FWOOM!

"AAAAAAAGH!"

Clayface cries out as his entire body is engulfed by fire. Flickering flames of red and orange lick around his limbs.

Within seconds Clayface gets baked like a piece of pottery. He's now a living clay sculpture, trapped in his own body!

An armored police truck pulls up next to the cooked criminal.

"Wait for him to cool off before you put him in the cooler," Robin tells Commissioner Gordon.

"Speaking of hot-heads ..." the Commissioner replies. "Where's Roland Daggett?"

Batman opens the Batmobile door. A frazzled Daggett climbs out.

Turn the page.

"The justice system gave you a second chance, Daggett," says the Dark Knight. "Try something different with your time and money."

"Choose wisely," Robin adds. "Or your past is sure to come back and haunt you!"

"I think I've seen and heard enough for one day," Daggett says. "I'm getting out of here."

"And what about you, Batman?" the Commissioner asks. "Usually you disappear after your work is done."

"Not this time," the Dark Knight answers. "Robin and I are going to stick around and see what other exciting things the World's Fair has to offer."

THE END

To follow another path, turn to page 16.

Batman drags the pretend Joker's form out of the trophy room.

Along the way, the villain spots a black umbrella on a nearby shelf. It's the trick umbrella that once belonged to The Penguin!

Clayface reaches out and grabs the weapon. He presses the button on the handle and a sharp blade extends from the tip.

ZING!

"En garde, Batman!" shouts Clayface. "I'm in the mood for some fowl play!"

The shape-shifter morphs into the Penguin and slashes at Batman. Batman whirls around and uses his cape as a shield. The blade slices through the fabric.

RIIIIIP!

The Penguin impostor lunges again, but Batman kicks the umbrella out of his grip. "Fwaughk!" squawks the Penguin. "Bad form, Batman!"

Turn the page.

Batman punches the Penguin square in the nose.

POW!

The troublemaker falls flat on his back. The pretend Penguin gets up and waddles back into the trophy room.

"Catch me if you can, Batman!" he cries.

Batman gives chase deeper into the gallery of gadgets and gizmos. He scans the area but sees no sign of Clayface.

SKRAASH!

Batman hears the smashing of glass and runs toward the sound.

Suddenly, he's confronted by his most frigid foe—Mr. Freeze!

"You've been holding out on me, Batman," Clayface says in Mr. Freeze's deep voice. "All the cool stuff is hidden in the back."

The fake Mr. Freeze reveals a long blaster from behind his back. It's his patented freeze ray! The dangerous device can shoot beams of ice, instantly freezing anything it touches.

"It's time to put you on ice, Batman!" he yells. The frozen fiend pulls the trigger just as Batman hurls a Batarang. It lodges in the gun's barrel, causing the weapon to backfire.

FWA-SHOOM!

The Dark Knight dives out of the way just as the freeze ray explodes in a shower of ice and snow.

When the debris settles, Batman finds a new addition has been added to his trophy room—Clayface trapped in a block of ice!

Turn the page.

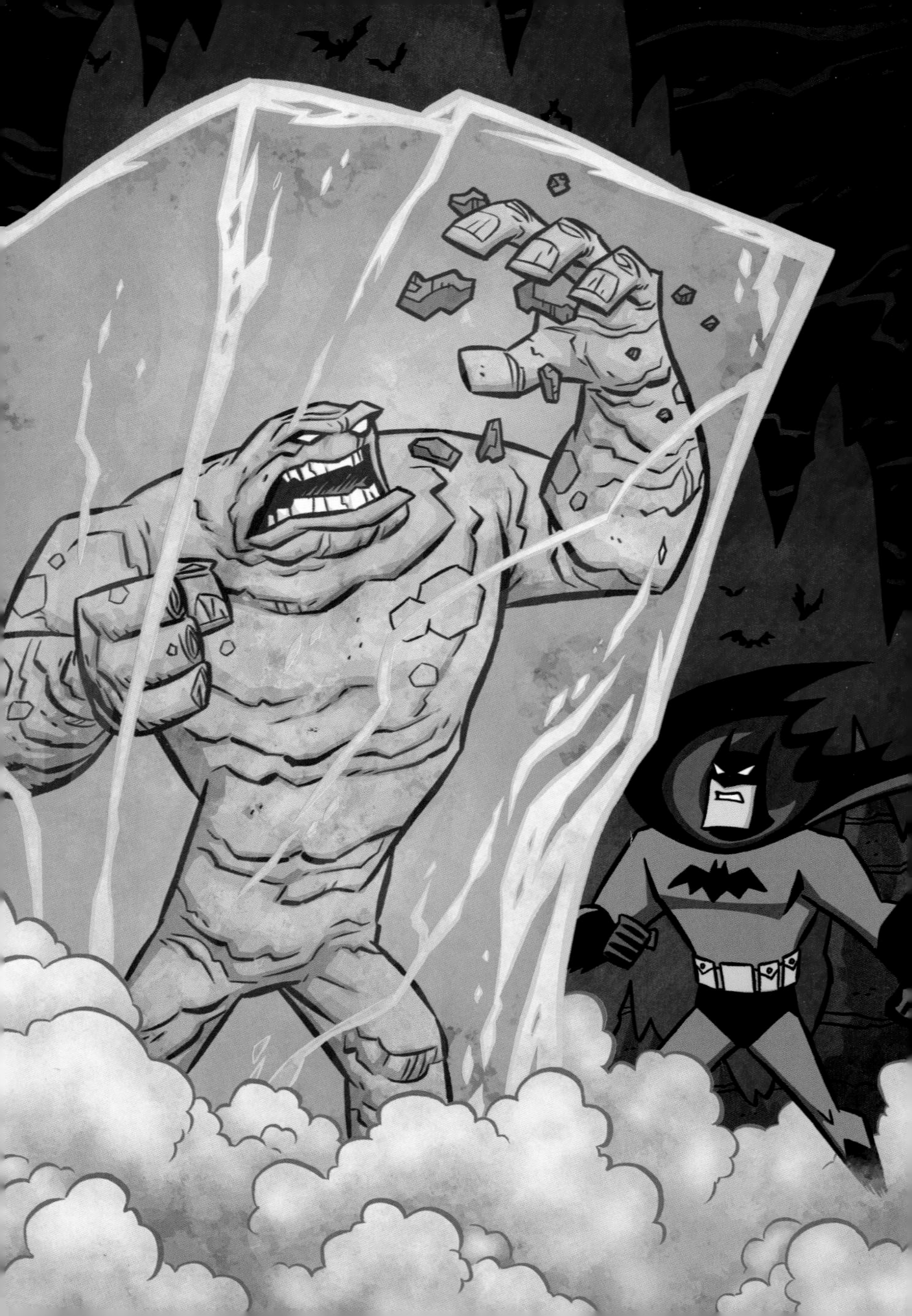

Alfred comes out of hiding and looks at the scary ice sculpture. "This garish ghoul won't be going on display in here will he, sir?" the butler asks.

"No. I think the best place for Clayface to thaw out would be in Arkham Asylum," Batman replies.

Just then Robin's face appears on the Batcomputer. He's calling from the World's Fair.

"Are you alright, Robin?" Batman asks.

"Yeah," he replies. "I've got good news and bad news. The good news is the Gray Ghost found me and helped me out."

Batman breathes a sigh of relief. "What's the bad news?" he asks.

"The Gray Ghost wants his car back!" Robin says.

Batman smiles. "I don't blame him," he says. "It certainly is, as you said before, a really sweet ride!"

THE END

To follow another path, turn to page 16.

AUTHOR

New York Times bestselling author John Sazaklis enjoys writing children's books about his favorite characters. He has also illustrated Spider-Man books and created toys used in *MAD* magazine. To him, it's a dream come true! John lives with his beautiful wife and daughter in New York City.

ILLUSTRATOR

Ethen Beavers lives and works in Modesto, California. He is best known for his work on the DC Super Friends Little Golden Book series at Random House, as well as the New York Times Bestselling series NERDS at Abrams publishing. He has also illustrated books and comics on titles like Samurai Jack, Batman, Star Wars, and Indiana Jones.

GLOSSARY

asylum (uh-SYE-lum)—a hospital for people who are mentally ill and cannot live by themselves

brute (BROOT)—a rough or violent person

corrupt (kuh-RUHPT)—willing to break laws to get money or power

impostor (im-POSS-tur)—someone who pretends to be something that he or she is not

pavilion (puh-VIL-yuhn)—an open building that is used for a show or an exhibit

projectile (pruh-JEK-tuhl)—an object, such as a bullet or missile, that is thrown or shot through the air

ransom (RAN-suhm)—money that is being demanded before someone who is being held captive is set free

revenge (ri-VENJ)—an action taken to repay for an injury or offense

silhouette (sil-oo-ET)—a dark outline seen against a light background

Utility Belt (yoo-TIL-uh-tee BELT)—Batman's belt, which holds all of his weaponry and gadgets

CLAYFACE

Real Name:
Matt Hagen

Occupation:
Professional Criminal

Base:
Gotham City

Height:
Varies

Weight:
Varies

Eyes:
Varies

Hair:
Varies

Formerly a big name in the movie industry, actor Matt Hagen had his face, and career, ruined in a tragic car crash. Hoping to regain his good looks, Hagen accepted the help of ruthless businessman Roland Daggett, who gave him a special cream that allowed Hagen to shape his face like clay. Hopelessly addicted, Hagen was caught stealing more cream, and Daggett forced him to consume an entire barrel as punishment. However, instead of killing Hagen, the large dose turned him into a monster with only one thing on his muddy mind—revenge.

- As Clayface, Matt Hagen is no longer human. His entire body is made of muddy clay, which grants him shape-shifting abilities as well as super-strength.

- Clayface's power is limited only by his imagination. He can turn his limbs into lethal weapons by willing his muddy body into whatever shape he desires.

- Everything Clayface does revolves around his relentless pursuit of Roland Daggett, the man who made him into a freak. Clayface will do whatever it takes to get Daggett within his muddy grasp, regardless of who is hurt or killed in the process.

- Drawing upon his shape-shifting abilities and his experience as an actor, Clayface assumes the shapes and voices of others. These abilities make him a very difficult foe to detect.

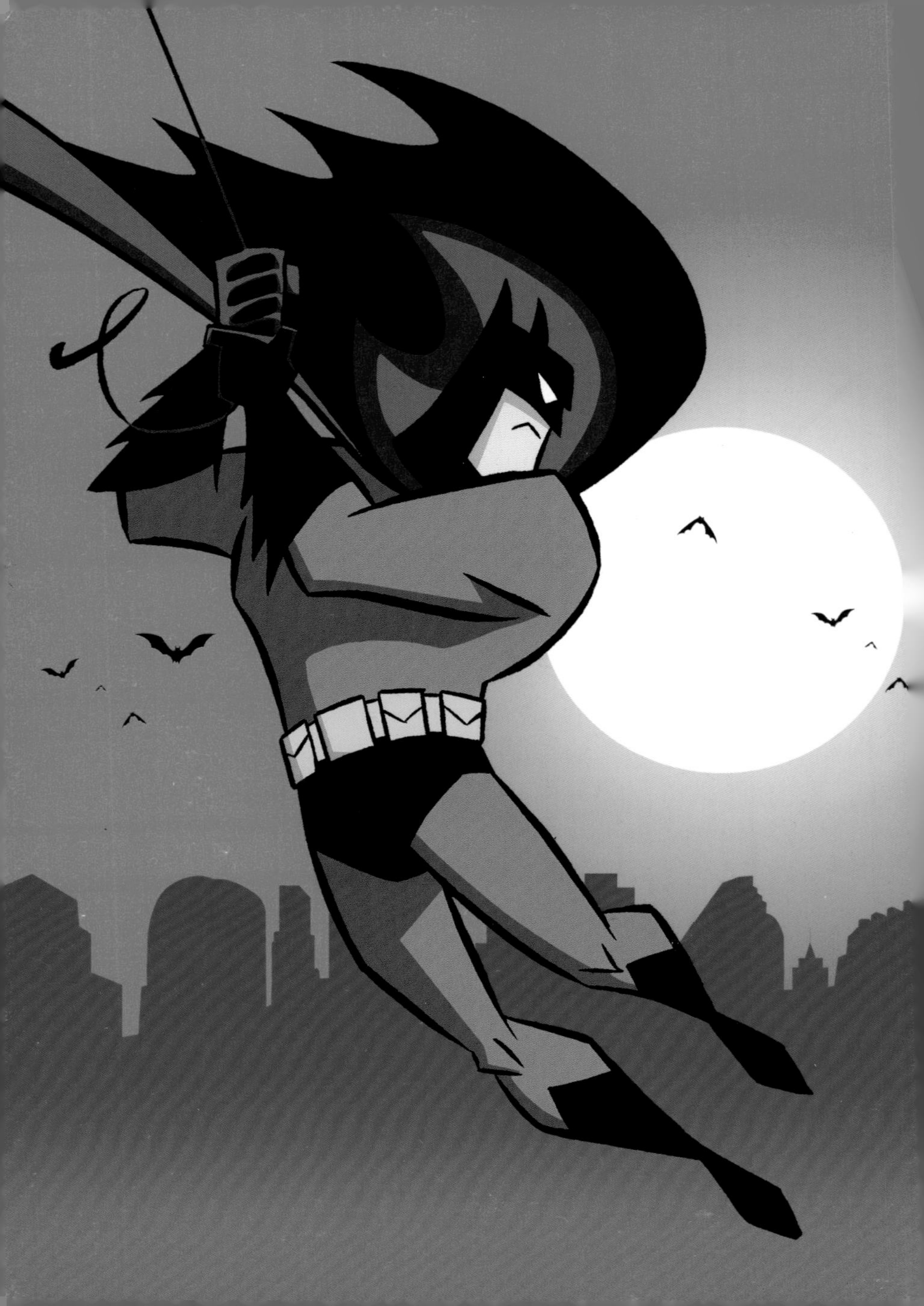

YOU CHOOSE

BATMAN™

IT'S YOUR TURN TO BE A SUPER HERO!

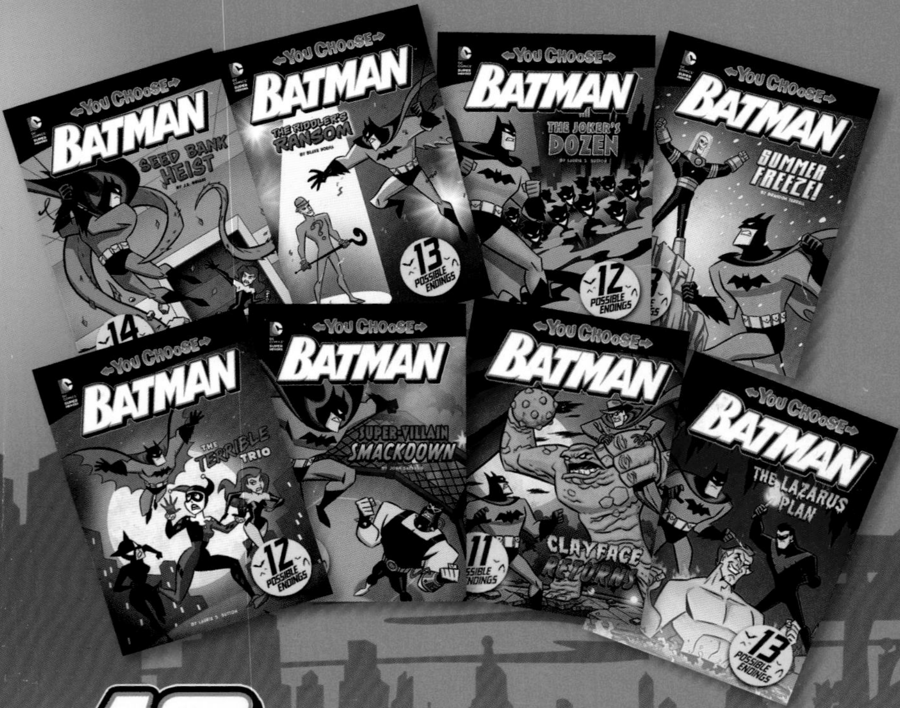

YOU CHOOSE
BATMAN
SEED BANK HEIST
YOU CHOOSE
BATMAN
THE RIDDLER'S RANSOM
13 POSSIBLE ENDINGS
YOU CHOOSE
BATMAN
THE JOKER'S DOZEN
12 POSSIBLE ENDINGS
YOU CHOOSE
BATMAN
SUMMER FREEZE!
YOU CHOOSE
BATMAN
THE TERRIBLE TRIO
12 POSSIBLE ENDINGS
YOU CHOOSE
BATMAN
SUPER-VILLAIN SMACKDOWN
YOU CHOOSE
BATMAN
CLAYFACE RETURNS
YOU CHOOSE
BATMAN
THE LAZARUS PLAN
13 POSSIBLE ENDINGS

10+ POSSIBLE ENDINGS!

THE FUN DOESN'T STOP HERE!

DISCOVER MORE AT...

WWW.CAPSTONEKIDS.COM

FIND COOL WEBSITES AND MORE BOOKS LIKE THIS ONE AT **WWW.FACTHOUND.COM.**

JUST TYPE IN THE BOOK ID: **9781496530899**

AND YOU'RE READY TO GO!

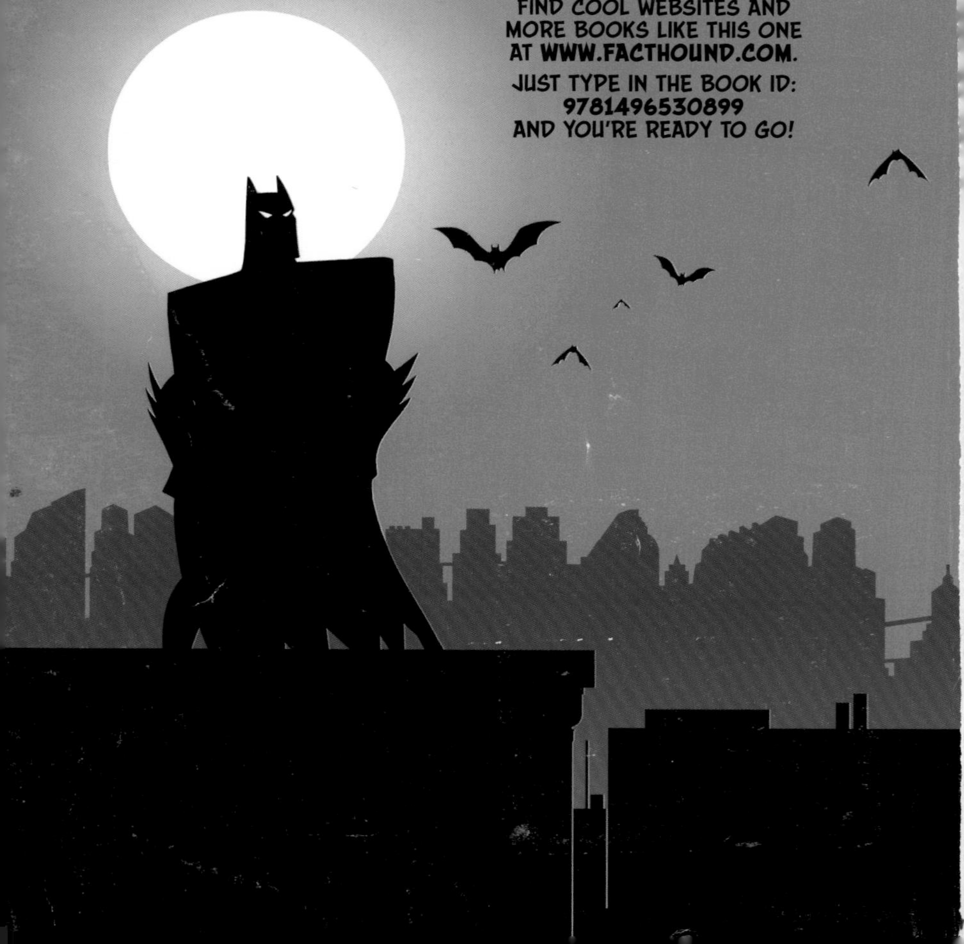